BUCKING THE SARGE

Also by Christopher Paul Curtis

BUD, NOT BUDDY

THE WATSONS GO TO BIRMINGHAM — 1963

BUCKING THE THE SARGE

CHRISTOPHER PAUL CURTIS

WENDY LAMB BOOKS

Published by
Wendy Lamb Books
an imprint of
Random House Children's Books
a division of Random House, Inc.
New York

Visit us on the Web! www.randomhouse.com/teens
Educators and librarians, for a variety of teaching tools, visit us at
www.randomhouse.com/teachers

Library of Congress Cataloging-in-Publication Data

Curtis, Christopher Paul.
Bucking the Sarge / Christopher Paul Curtis
p.   cm.
Summary: Deeply involved in his cold and manipulative mother's shady business
dealings in Flint, Michigan, fourteen-year-old Luther keeps a sense of humor while
running the Happy Neighbor Group Home For Men, all the while dreaming of going to
college and becoming a philosopher.
ISBN 0-385-32307-7 (trade) — ISBN 0-385-90159-3 (lib. bdg.) [1. Business enterprises—
Fiction. 2. Fraud—Fiction. 3. Group homes—Fiction. 4. Mothers—Fiction. 5. People
with mental disabilities—Fiction. 6. African Americans—Fiction. 7. Flint (Mich.)—
Fiction.] I. Title.
PZ7.C94137Bw 2004

[Fic]—dc22   2004006445
Printed in the United States of America

September 2004

10 9 8 7 6 5 4 3 2 1

BVG

To Shakira Chantelle Wilson and
Darnell Lee Wilson
And to the memory of my dear Uncle Sterling June Sleet

Many thanks to the following people who read the book and offered valuable suggestions:

Elaine Astles, Kay Benjamin, Pauletta Bracy, Steven Curtis, Terry Fisher, Dante Gatti, John Jarvey, Teri Lesesne, Edward Langstone, Megann Licskai, Blake Lundy, Mona Lundy, Kendra Patrick, Barb Perris, Alison Root, Traki Taylor and Mickial Wilson, Uncle Bullethead. And especially to WL, Eunice Blatt.

MY LIFE LISTING

"Luther T. Farrell, you *got* to be more careful."

Sparky climbed into the front seat and slapped something brown and squarish on the dashboard of my ride.

My wallet!

My hand flew to the back of my jeans and patted the pocket where my wallet was supposed to have been. Stupid. I know.

I snatched my wallet and opened it to see if anything was missing. I felt like I'd been gut-punched. Except for one thing, it was completely empty.

"Aw, man, someone jacked me! Where'd you get it?"

"On the floor in Mrs. Bohannon's lab."

I'd been in Mrs. Bohannon's lab after my last class. She'd been trying to help me develop a knockout science fair project and she was almost as excited about it as I was. If I came up with a great idea I'd be the first student ever to win the science fair for three years in a row at Whittier Middle School. And probably the first at any school in Flint.

It had to be one of those chemistry geeks who'd picked my pocket! I bet it was that Lucas Sorge.

Sparky said, "You know what, Luther, I didn't think it was possible, but if word of this gets out your reputation will sink even lower than it was before. You know everybody already thinks there's something wrong with you the way you stress out over that science fair, but if I let people know you lost your wallet you wouldn't just be known as a wannabe brainiac, you'd have the rep for being a *absentminded* wannabe brainiac."

"Sparky, this isn't any time to be joking around, I'ma be in some big trouble."

Sparky said, "And ever since you were in Pampers who is it that's had your back? Who's been there with you through the fire, to the limit, to the wall . . ."

I tuned Sparky out and started worrying about what my mother, aka the Sarge, was gonna say when she found out all my stuff had been ripped off. No, let me break that down; it wasn't what she was gonna say that had me worried, it was what she was gonna *do*. The Sarge's discipline techniques aren't the kind of thing you'd learn on the Parenting Network, they're more like what you'd pick up from watching the Animal Channel.

Sparky kept running his mouth: ". . . but I don't expect any thanks, it's just another case of me selflessly bailing my boy out."

I said, "How're you bailing me out? How's you giving me a empty wallet supposed to be bailing me out?"

2

"It wasn't completely empty."

Here it comes. Sparky was about to say something about the only thing the thief had left in my wallet.

I'm not ashamed, I'm not trying to hide anything, it was a condom. To be real, it was the oldest condom on the face of the earth. It'd been in my wallet so many years that I'd had to give it a name—I called it Chauncey. Chauncey and that wallet had spent so much time together that it would've been a crime to separate them, not that there was any chance of that happening anytime soon. They'd been together so long that Chauncey had wore a circle right in the leather, and a circle ain't nothing but a great big zero, which was just about my chances of ever busting Chauncey loose and using him.

I said, "Man, the Sarge's gonna kill me."

Sparky said, "Maybe it's not as bad as you think, maybe this'll help."

He snapped his fingers like a magician and a card appeared.

I took it from him. "It figures. My library card, what's a thief gonna do with a library card?"

Sparky said, "I can understand why they left you that, but what I don't get is why they left that condom. Old as that baby is, I bet they could've got some good money from a museum for it."

Sparky snapped his fingers again. This time my driver's license appeared.

Whew! The Sarge had had to pull some serious strings to get me that, if I'da had to go apply for another one it wouldn'ta been good.

3

Sparky started reading from my license: "Height: six foot four, weight a hundred thirty-five." He snorted and said, "Yeah, maybe if you had twenty pounds of quarters in your pockets. And here's something I don't get, if I'm a few months older than you and I'm only fifteen, how come this license says you're eighteen?"

Even though I treat Sparky like a brother, the Sarge taught me that there are some things that aren't *anybody* else's business. I said, "Connections, my brother, connections."

Sparky said, "I guess so."

He snapped again and read from the piece of paper that magically appeared in his hand. It was the title to my ride. "Yeah, you really would need some serious connections to be fifteen years old and have a eighty-five-thousand-dollar ride that's already paid off."

He shook his head and handed me my title.

He snapped again. This finger popping was starting to get old, but at least every time he did it it meant I was getting something back.

Sparky was holding three credit cards.

Oh, snap! Sparky handed me my JCPenney's card, my Platinum MasterCard and my American Express Gold Card.

That was just about everything, just about. I waited for another pop.

Sparky was torturing me. Finally he snapped again and a fifty-dollar bill was in his fingers. It wasn't what I was really looking for, but fifty bucks is fifty bucks. It was my emergency money. He handed it to me and said, "I know I'm supposed to be your boy, and I know we swore to have

4

each other's backs from womb to tomb, from birth to earth, but after going through your wallet I gotta let you know something, my brother."

"What's that?"

"You need to quit all that whining about how rough your life is."

I said, "Look who's talking."

"Naw, Luther, I'm for real."

I told him, "Buckle your seat belt, Sparky, you know I gotta pick up my crew by four."

Sparky buckled his belt as I pulled away from the curb. I always parked a few blocks away from the school.

We'd had this conversation about who was better off before. We look at things in different ways but we always stay tight.

Sparky's been my main dog since kindergarten. His real name is Dewey but he outgrew that around second grade.

His father used to be a fireman and since their crib was just around the corner from the firehouse, his dad let him walk down there after school and polish the bell and do other cool things all the time.

After his dad got shot the other firemen still let Sparky hang around and always had something for him to do.

Darnell Dixon, the Sarge's go-to guy and my boss and one of Flint's leading psychopath nut jobs, had told Dewey, "It's a crying shame the way they treat you down at that fire station, youngblood. Word is that the way you hang out there so much they think of you like some kind of little mascot. Fact is they been calling you Sparky the Fire Dog behind your back."

That's one reason I have so much respect for Sparky. Darnell called himself trying to be hateful but Sparky flipped the script on him. He took the name and wore it with honor. He was proud of the firemen because they always made him feel at home and mostly because they reminded him of his pops, so from the time he was seven years old he made everyone call him Sparky.

I turned left onto Court Street.

Sparky said, "Naw, Luther, you got it straight-up made. Stop and think about it, you know how you always making them lists for everything you're gonna do and everything you want to do? If I sat down and made my own list of the top one hundred things that I'd ever wanted in life you'd already have ninety-eight of them."

Sparky started ticking things off on his fingers. "One, you're toting all that plastic around and I know that AmEx card don't even have a limit; two, you got your own vehicle; three, you got a for-real, honest-to-God, straight from the Secretary of State phony driver's license that says you're eighteen when we both know you're only fifteen—and a immature fifteen at that; four, you kiss every teacher in school's behind and get good grades; five, you carry fifty bucks in your wallet at all times; six, your momma owns half the ghetto; seven, she's got them group homes; eight, she's got so much cash she lends money out like a bank; nine, you got six million dollars she set aside in that education fund . . ."

I interrupted, "Being real it's ninety-two thousand, five hundred and ten dollars, and that's ninety-two thousand, five hundred and ten dollars for more than two years of eighty-hour weeks."

6

Sparky said, "Whatever, Number ten, she bought that bad fifty-three-inch plasma TV. . . ." Sparky ran out of fingers so he started slapping the dashboard. "Eleven . . ."

Bam!

". . . she had Darnell Dixon hook you up with that free satellite; twelve . . ."

Bam!

". . . don't no one care if you watch high-definition cartoons from sunup to sundown; thirteen . . ."

Bam!

". . . you're gonna inherit all them things from her, and that's just the start. You got it all, baby."

I rolled my eyes.

Sparky said, "Of course you do have a couple things going on that wouldn't make my list."

I said, "A couple? How 'bout having to look after a bunch of grown men twenty-four seven?"

Sparky said, "And for number two, the way you have to clean those dudes up and change some of their diapers."

I said, "And three, having to work all day Saturday and Sunday and from four till midnight every other night."

Sparky said, "And four, when it comes to basketball you're a waste of six-feet-and-four-inches."

I said, "And five, having to make sure my crew gets shaved, dressed, washed up, medicated, driven to the rehab center, and driven to their doctors' appointments and therapy sessions. Then there's prepping and painting the rental houses for new tenants, and cleaning the—"

Sparky said, "And six, there's the thing about you not being exactly the best-looking brother in Flint."

Sparky was on a roll, but he was wrong there. I've always thought of myself as being handsome, but in a unusual sort of way. And if that Clearasil really works it won't be too much longer before I'll be handsome in a more normal sense of the word.

Sparky said, "Then seven, there's the fact that you ain't never had a woman, and probably never will."

I said, "And eight, the fact that . . . wait a minute, you're trying to say I've *never* had a woman?"

Sparky looped his thumb and pointing finger in a circle and said, "N'e'en one, *nada*, baby."

I said, "So you mean to tell me your momma had a sex-change operation? I knew there was something strange about her."

Sparky laughed and said, "I know *you* don't want to start panning on folks' mothers, do you?"

He had me there. When it comes to having your mother talked about I'm wide open to being abused. I changed the subject.

"What about you, Sparky? You're the one who's got it made and doesn't know it."

"Wha-a-at?"

"Let me break one of my patented Luther T. Farrell lists down for you. Number one, you don't have someone standing over you all the time telling you what to do —"

Sparky interrupted, "Two, I got no funds, I got no job."

I said, "Three, you can come and go anytime you want to —"

"Four, I got no clothes, I got no shoes."

8

I said, "Five, you come to school only if you feel like it —"

Sparky said, "Six, half my meals are at your place and I'm eating that same garbage you serve them people you look after —"

I said, "Seven, you got me as your best friend."

Sparky trumped the whole conversation: "Eight through two hundred forty-seven thousand, I live in Flint."

I don't mean to say my boy is obsessed, but Sparky blames all our problems on the fact that we live in Flint. Yeah, I'm looking to get out someday myself, but this is one of those things that me and Sparky don't think alike on. But that's not his fault. My mind is trained in a different way than his.

I like to look at everything philosophically, and he doesn't. I've known since I was about six that thinking that way will get you what you need in life so I've been studying philosophical junk since then.

It gets a laugh every time I tell someone but by the time I'm twenty-one I plan on being America's best-known, best-loved, best-paid philosopher. And that's a job that there's gotta be a big demand for 'cause how many full-time, famous, professional American philosophers can you think of?

I rest my case.

It's because of the way my mind is trained that I don't join everybody else coming down on Flint so tough. Flint ain't nothing but a place or a state of mind, and I think a place or a state of mind is all about what you make it to be.

But not Sparky, he *knows* that if he lived somewhere flashy like Gary, Indiana, or New Orleans or New York City he'd be sitting pretty.

I pulled into the parking lot of the Genesee County Adult Rehabilitation Center and hit the horn.

My crew was standing just inside the front door. They picked up their lunch pails, hooked arms, and started walking to where me and Sparky were parked. There are only four men in my crew right now. We're down from the usual eight. The Sarge was having trouble filling spots because the other group homes in the area didn't have the amount of rejects and last-chance cases they usually send to us.

I opened the door and Mr. Foster was the first to get in. He's the leader of the pack. Before he got sick he was a top dog with some insurance company. Now he spends his days dogging the rest of the Crew, watching television and reminding me how bad my life is.

He said, "Gentlemen, good to see you both." We had finally got his medications tuned so that he didn't have the big mood swings.

Mr. Baker was next. He's the official Happy Neighbor Group Home for Men grumpy old man, nicotine addict and pyromaniac. Medications don't do a thing to him.

He'd been holding his breath since I pulled up and now that he was in he let out a lungful of cigarette smoke all over me.

He put his hand over his mouth and said, "Was that me?"

He knew how much I hated breathing in smoke. He wasn't supposed to be smoking but someone at the center

10

would give him cigarettes if he promised not to cause any trouble.

One of the rehab center's aides helped in the last two of my crew, Mr. Keller and Mr. Hart, and buckled their belts.

Mr. Keller has to be kept loaded up on a ton of meds, it's the only way we can keep him from going off on folks. He's so far out of it that Mr. Foster calls him Dial Tone.

Mr. Hart is helpless. He should've been in the Sarge's chronic care home but his people had enough cash to pay the Sarge a little extra something and have him stay with me. They told the Sarge it was worth it 'cause they liked the care I gave the men.

And I do take pride in the way I look after my crew. It's a lot of responsibility and I've been pretty much in charge of the Happy Neighbor Group Home for Men since I was thirteen, but I gotta tell you, ever since I'd had that first good feeling and excitement about being in charge of something it's been a two-and-a-half-year downhill slide.

"Everybody buckled?"

Sparky said, "Hold on."

He snapped his fingers one more time and the last thing that was missing from my wallet appeared.

Sparky looked at it and said, "The Methuselah condom says 'sad,' but I gotta tell you, bruh, this is even worse. You need to stand in line and get you your capital 'P,' which stands for 'pathetic,' 'cause that's what this is shouting. How long you been carrying this thing around?"

He handed it to me.

It was a picture of the woman I'm doomed to love and

11

hate for the rest of my life, Shayla Dawn of the Dead Patrick.

Sparky was right, this was pathetic. It was Shayla's fourth-grade school picture. I'd wanted a more recent one but fourth grade was the last time me and the love of my life had had a conversation that didn't end with us wanting to scratch each other's eyes out.

What could I say? I asked Sparky, "Where you say they're passing out them capital 'P's?"

He shook his head and said, "Like a brother like me would know."

He scrambled into the back, sat next to Mr. Foster and said, "Go 'head, everyone's buckled."

I put the DVD in and the first notes from *The Lion King* echoed around as I pulled out onto Atherton Road.

Welcome to the life and times of Luther T. Farrell. A lot of unphilosophical minds think just like Sparky, they think I'm sitting fat, but what do they know? Sometimes you don't know the true story until you've lived it. I've lived it. And believe me, some of the time the truth ain't pretty.

· 2 ·

"SO LONG, SEW-CRATES"

The next day the phone rang.

I checked the caller ID.

"What's up, Sparky?"

He said, "You in the dayroom?"

"Yeah."

"Quick, turn them cartoons off and switch over to channel five, that commercial is 'bout to come on!"

"Hold on."

I picked up the remote and changed to channel 5. The credits for one of the stories were just rolling by.

Mr. Baker said, "Hey!"

I told him, "Just a minute, Mr. Baker, Sparky's been telling me about this commercial for weeks and after I see it we'll go back."

Mr. Baker said, "Well, it better be a quick one."

I told Sparky, "I got it."

"OK, check him out and see if I was lying," Sparky said. "This brother is going to be my one-way ticket out of Flint."

The commercial started with a shot of this old woman walking in front of a camera shop on a windy, wintry day. She hit a patch of ice, and before you could blink, she was five feet up in the air. She landed, making a cracking noise, and began moaning. Her left leg was twisted up so bad it looked like part of it had broke off. Next you could see some guy in a big old 'fro peek out from the curtains of the camera store right before his hand stuck a Out of Business sign on the window.

The next shot was of Sparky's "dog," a brother sitting on the edge of a desk with a shelf full of thick, serious-looking books behind him. I'd seen the suit he was wearing at Sleet-Sterling, it was a Versace with a three-and-a-half-G price tag.

He said, "Tired of them doing something negligent, then laughing in your face when all you ask is to be treated fairly?"

The next scene was of a man working in a factory screwing bolts into something with his face all twisted up like he was constipated. He took his gloves off and began rubbing his wrist. Then a white man in a shirt and tie was standing over his shoulder foaming at the mouth and yelling for the brother to get back at the bolts.

The camera came in close as a tiny tear dripped out of the worker's eye while the boss kept yelling, "You're slowing things down—move! Move! Moooove!"

Sparky's dog, looking as sad and serious as ever, was

back on. The camera moved a little closer to him as he jabbed a finger at us and said, "Tired of them ignoring your pain and putting unbearable, unfair stress on you?"

The next shot showed a woman sitting in a restaurant talking to a man while she ate a bowl of soup. The man dropped his fork, bugged his eyes out of his head and pointed at the woman's spoon. There, kicking away like it was doing the backstroke, was the front end of a roach that must've been the size of a paperback novel. It was hard to tell, though, because where the back half of the roach was supposed to have been you couldn't see nothing but the woman's teeth marks.

The camera moved in closer and closer on the roach while the woman looked like . . . well, like anyone would look if they just found out they were chewing on a giant cockroach's booty.

Sparky's dog was back on. He said, "Tired of them not giving you the respect you deserve? Tired of those jackasses having the last laugh when it comes down to justice being served? Well, so am I."

He got up off the desk and crossed his arms and stood like he was Superman. He picked up a long black strap and dangled it from his right hand.

"My name's attorney Dontay Orlando Gaddy and my initials spell 'D.O.G.' and you call me and tell me what happened and I promise you I will be on them like an American Staffordshire terrier, which is just a fancy name for a pit bull. And remember, big or small . . ."

The camera jumped closer to Dontay Orlando Gaddy.

He said, ". . . I will . . ."

A drum banged as the camera jerked in closer.

". . . sue . . ."

The drum banged again. Whoever was filming this must've just learned how to use the zoom lens—they were wearing it out.

". . . 'em . . ."

Another boom and Dontay's face took up the whole screen:

". . . all!"

The camera pulled back as Dontay Orlando Gaddy slapped the strap he was holding against his desk. It sounded like a roll of thunder.

The next shot was of the camera shop dude in the big old 'fro, the boss in the shirt and tie and some brother in a white jacket and a cook's hat standing together wearing handcuffs. All their pockets had been turned inside out like they'd been jacked and they were scowling with their lips stuck out. Then the commercial showed the old lady with bad balance, the worker with weak wrists and the roach-eating woman standing together counting big rolls of cash while the American flag waved in the wind and a band played "God Bless America."

An announcer said, "Attorney Dontay Orlando Gaddy is on our side, and remember, big or small, he will sue 'em all! Call 1-800-SUE-EM-ALL for a no-charge consultation! Get everything you deserve!"

The announcer repeated the number four more times.

Sparky was screaming into the phone, "What'd I tell you? Is he bad or what?"

I said, "Yeah, your boy is something else."

"I told you! I'ma get him on my side, I'ma find me someone to sue!"

"Good luck."

"All right then, I'll catch you later."

"Cool. Peace."

I hung up.

I could tell that Mr. Baker was starting to fiend for a cigarette. His eyes were glued to the television and his hands were bouncing to the same beat as the drum in Dontay Orlando Gaddy's commercial.

He said, "Sue 'em all! Sue 'em all! Sue 'em all!"

Just like that the room was filled with four men all waving their arms and chanting the Dontay Gaddy theme, "Sue 'em all! Sue 'em all! Sue 'em all!" Even Mr. Foster was joining in, trying to get everyone worked up.

I picked up the phone to call Sparky so he could listen to what he'd started but I heard a car pull up into the driveway.

I looked out the window and saw the Sarge and Darnell Dixon getting out of his white-on-white-in-white with white leather, fully loaded, three-month-old Buick Riviera with the personalized license plates that said HI BABY.

Uh-oh! This was all I needed, for the Sarge to walk in here and find the Crew chanting about taking someone to court. As much trouble as she used to have with lawsuits, she'd kill me for putting ideas in her clients' heads.

I hung up, grabbed the remote and punched the cartoon channel back on. *Scooby-Doo!*'s theme music was playing and I jumped in front of the television and yelled, "Scoo-Bee-Doo! Scoo-Bee-Doo! Scoo-Bee-Doo!"

17

By the time the Sarge and Darnell Dixon came into the dayroom to see what the ruckus was about I was back in my chair and the Crew was locked in chanting, "Scoo-Bee-Doo! Scoo-Bee-Doo! Scoo-Bee-Doo!"

The Sarge saw the four of them, then looked at me and said, "After you unload the supplies come into my office, looks like it's time we reviewed everyone's medication again."

I kept a straight face and said, "OK," but inside I was dying laughing.

This is another one of those types of things that I look at philosophically, especially everything dealing with the Sarge. It reminds me of what a great philosopher, whose name escapes me at the moment, once said: "Laugh and the world laughs with you," but the philosopher forgot to put in, "as long as the Sarge doesn't find out."

That's one of the reasons that when I go off to university I'ma dedicate my life to studying philosophy—it can answer just about any question that you might have. Plus, if you don't have a stable, lucid, nonmoneygrubbing adult in your life who can give you decent advice, philosophy can be a pretty good substitute.

It took me a while when I was young to know how important philosophy is. I stayed away from it because so many philosophers have those long, foreign, impossible-to-pronounce names. That can be kind of embarrassing if you're having a conversation and you want to throw in a philosopher's name to try to sound a little more intelligent than you are.

I can never forget the pain and heartache that scarred

the emotions of a certain young, naive philosophy lover, whose name we won't call, when his burned-out old teacher'd said, "I've never heard of a thirteen-year-old being so interested in philosophy, why do you like it so much?"

The student had stroked his chin like he had a bad little goatee going and said, "Now, I can't be exactly sure if it was Sew-crates or Ar-is-totally who said, 'The unexamined life is not worth living.'"

The teacher looked confused. "Who said that?"

The poor student repeated the names.

The teacher gave a hating smile and only halfway tried not to die laughing. "I believe they're pronounced 'Sah-cruh-tees' and 'Air-is-tott-ul.'"

After something like that all your credibility is shot. Stand in line and get your capital "I" 'cause that's what you look like, a giant idiot.

I learned to say, "This reminds me of what that great philosopher, whose name escapes me at the moment, once said. . . ." It keeps your conversation flowing along real nice.

That's why you'll never find Luther T. Farrell looking down on somebody just because they have a little trouble with the pronunciation of a messed-up name. Another reason why it's easy to see that Luther T. Farrell has found a home in science and a haven in philosophy.

· 3 ·

CHESTER X

The next day the Sarge said, in a voice deeper than mine, "I don't have to spell it out for you, do I? Your teachers have always said what a bright boy you are, and you do have that unusual knack for philosophy, so why should I have to draw pictures for you in regards to something as simple as this?"

I let her sarcastic remark about philosophy slide right by me and looked over at the dried-up little surprise that was waiting in the bed across the room from mine.

I asked her, "How come he's gotta stay in my room? Why can't we move him in with Mr. Baker?"

She was in a pretty good mood—she decided to give me an answer. It was weak, but it was an answer.

She patted the man's medication chart, which to her is kind of like putting your hand on the Bible, and said, "This is a special case, we need to take extra care to make sure everything's properly documented and thoroughly charted with him."

Which translated into English that nothing could look fishy if this old dude died.

I looked back at her. She was staring. "Need I say more?"

She gave me that look that was supposed to let me peer into the depths of her soul. I don't know what I was supposed to see when I looked there, but whatever it was it sure didn't seem deep and it didn't have anything to do with soul.

I said, "No."

Her left eyebrow arched in a way that I'd practiced for years but couldn't quite do. She said, "No?"

I said, "I mean 'No, you don't have to say anything more.'"

"Good." And she was gone. I hope she headed back over to her place.

I bent over to get a good look at this little old man.

His eyes were closed and his eyeballs were moving side to side under lids that couldn't've been more than two or three molecules thick. Even though the rest of him was perfectly still, those roving eyeballs made it seem like he was looking hard for someone. Or like he was being chased by something and couldn't tell from which direction it was about to snatch him.

I picked up the medication chart that hung from a nail in the footboard of his bed. "Chester X Stockard" was written across the top. His name was followed by five "A"s.

Snap! I'd never seen anyone with more than three be-fore. The "A"s were a part of the Sarge's chart code to show what kind of cash, benefits and insurance each of her clients had. This old man must be loaded.

Then I got why the Sarge was so interested in him. Right under his name, in the next-of-kin box, was a big fat zero.

The Sarge had said this guy was somewhere on the wrong side of eighty. I checked him out closer and this def-initely wasn't what I thought eighty years of banging around on Earth would leave someone looking like.

His skin was stretched so smooth and tight across his face that it seemed like someone had tied weights to his ears. He didn't have a bit of fat showing on his half-bald head, which wasn't even putting a dent in the pillow, and judging by the little bumps and knobs that were sticking up under the covers, there wasn't too much meat on this old bird anywhere.

The only things that might make you think that he had some serious miles on his odometer were the thick little white hairs sticking out of his chin and upper lip. They looked kind of cool against his brown skin, but they didn't fit. It was easy to see if he was up-and-at-'em he wouldn't put up with having this stubble growing on him. He seemed like the kind of person who cared about how he looked. Sort of like me.

Two weeks ago the Sarge had told me she was working on getting a "special client" who needed "special care" and would be staying in my room. I wasn't too happy about getting a roommate but I'd already had a chance to get over being mad about it. I went to the bathroom and got a load of things so I could start making this old-timer a little more presentable.

I tucked a towel under his chin and gave his beard a good soapy wash. His eyes never stopped moving under the veiny lids. I shot some shaving cream into my hand and started massaging it into his face. The tiny white bristles tickled my palm.

Someday I'll be doing this on my own face. Now I've got exactly six sorry hairs growing under my chin, which might sound like a lot, but they're as soft and skinny as cat fur. Darnell Dixon had told me if you shave them off they come back twice as thick and twice as quick, but so far all the shaving had got me was a crop of nasty bumps and little pimples with six cat hairs growing out from the middle of them.

I imagined what it would be like to trade places with this Chester X Stockard dude if only so I could have the thick stubbly beard he had covering his cheeks, but then I checked myself.

I remembered what that old philosopher, whose name escapes me at the moment, once said: "Be careful about what you wish for because you just might get it."

Most times I'd wish I was someone or something or somewhere else. I'd be sitting in history class looking out the window and, stupid as it sounds, I'd start getting jealous of a blue jay hopping in the grass out behind the school.

I'd think, "Bird, you don't know how good you've got it,

no teachers to deal with, no girls worrying you to death, or, let's be real, no *lack* of girls worrying you to death, and best of all, no Sarge."

But as usual, I came back to my senses, especially when I started thinking about how long a blue jay could live. Between cats and winter and their nasty, stressed-out attitude, it doesn't seem like a blue jay's gonna last more than five or six years, and at eighty years old how much more time could this Chester X Stockard have left on Earth? When you add in the fact that it looked like the Sarge had started the countdown to his final days, trading places didn't seem like such a good idea after all. Even if he did have five "A"s after his name. Even if he did have a billion thick little hairs popping out all over his chin and cheeks.

I checked my feelings of envy and dipped the razor in the basin of water.

I started at his Adam's apple and began slowly scraping the razor toward his chin. I'd shaved a million of the Sarge's clients before and most of them were so old or slack-faced from their meds that the skin around their necks was like a soft, wadded-up blanket that had been sewn to the bottoms of their jawbones, but this Chester X Stockard's neck was just as firm and tight as mine. Shaving him was gonna be easy.

I thought for a second if I should let him start growing a mustache, then decided the hair on his lip had to go too. I held back and checked out my good work.

The Sarge would've been proud. One of her biggest no-nos is that one of her clients would show some sign that something physical had happened to him. With the troubles we'd had before, she was big on making sure that they didn't have any bruises, scrapes or cuts that might get infected and could be seen as a sign of neglect or abuse. When the times came that we had no choice but to get physical with one of the clients we had to be good and sure that it wasn't on the face or the arms.

That's why she taught me the Happy Neighbor Group Home finger curl. What you do is put your fingers on top of the client's and roll your fingers into their palm. The pain it gives is so tough that you can have someone jumping around like SpongeBob SquarePants on speed, and it doesn't leave any kind of mark.

From studying about philosophy I'd learned about something called karma, where whatever you do in this life, good or bad, comes back on you twice as much in your next life. In the Happy Neighbor Group Home for Men the Sarge has got her own version of karma: if you put a visible mark on one of her clients she puts the same mark on you times five, and there isn't any waiting around till your next life to get the payback, either, you get yours right away.

I put the razor on Chester X Stockard's lip to swipe away the last bit of lather, and wouldn't you know it, his mouth twitched and he made a little kissing sound.

A drop of blood began leaking from his lip. I set the razor down and took the washcloth and rinsed and wiped his face. Then I picked up the roll of toilet paper I'd brought in, tore a small corner off of one of the sheets and stuck it on the nick. Except for the tiny, bloody speck of toilet paper on his face, this was a big improvement.

I said, "Well, Pops, if you've gotta hang out here till the

grim reaper comes knocking, at least you won't be looking bummish when he grabs you."

His eyes snapped open.

I tried to be cool but I'd seen too many scary flicks that started just like this. My neck hairs jumped up and I took a step back.

He finally said, "Oh. Oh, it's you. I didn't know I was back."

I was glad his meds had kept him still for ninety-nine percent of the shave. I pulled myself together and patted the hand he'd started waving around. It was shaky and veiny and twisted-up and knobby, looking like a brown baby bird moving its head from side to side.

"That's right," I said, "you're back, now just chill and try to go back to sleep."

There were two hazy gray rings creeping into the brownness of his eyeballs, sort of like two scoops of chocolate ice cream were slowly dissolving in a couple of glasses of yellowish-gray milk.

He tried to focus his eyes on me and finally it seemed he could tell he didn't know who I was.

He grumbled a little and said, "Let me ask you this, young man"—his mouth kept moving even after the words had stopped coming out—"do you think you understand white people?"

Huh? Where'd that come from? I couldn't help laughing. I said, "No. But I can't say I ever really tried."

His eyes closed again. "Good, if you ever think you do, you mark that day on a calendar 'cause then you can go

26

back and know that that was the day you made one of the biggest mistakes of your life."

"I'll do that."

He kept his eyes closed. "And what about us? Do you think you understand black folks?"

I thought for a second. "That's a definite no to that one."

He smiled and that was enough to make the tiny piece of red and white toilet paper flutter off his lip. "Well," he said, "God must still be good, 'cause you're a lot smarter than you look."

A spike of Valium or Demerol or whatever the Sarge was using on Chester X Stockard must've shot through his heart—just like that he was out as cold as before.

Good thing for him, too, I know when I've been insulted and if I had, say, two or three days to think about it I probably would've been able to come back with something to put him in his place.

But things like this don't bother me that much anymore. From dealing with Mr. Baker I've had lots of practice being insulted by the Sarge's clients and have learned you've got to ignore them. Most times they don't know what they're saying. It'd take more than something that whack to get to me, I've been insulted by the best. I'm not one to unnecessarily brag, but I've even stood up to the Sarge and come away smiling.

Most times we keep the TV in the dayroom on the 24 Hour Cartoon Channel for the clients and I'm not ashamed to admit that a lot of my love of philosophy has come from

27

there. When it comes to being dissed I'm just like my boy Batfink. Right before someone's about to open up on him with a Tec nine he wraps his gigantic wings around his body and says, "Your bullets cannot harm me, my wings are like a shield of steel." And sure enough, the hood's bullets bounce off Batfink like hail off a sidewalk.

When the Sarge or Darnell Dixon or some fool at school is jumping all over me, trying to make me feel bad, I put on my game face and keep saying to myself, "Your words cannot harm me, my mind is like a shield of steel," and all the negativity and hate-eration ricochet off me and float into space, as harmless as sunshine.

I looked back at Chester X Stockard. Nice try, old man, but you're gonna have to do a lot better than that to get to Luther T. Farrell.

I poured a little extra of that stinging aftershave on the cut on his lip.

Not to be mean, but to help him learn a lesson that anyone who was going to be living in a group home needs to learn: Getting mouthy seconds before you lapse into un-consciousness is a pretty bad idea. Tell me that doesn't sound philosophical!

· 4 ·

"BREAK A RULE, LOSE YOUR ALLOWANCE . . ."

My study of philosophy has taught me that there really are certain advantages to having the coldhearted, moneygrubbing, beastly sadist who runs your life be blessed with a good vocabulary and a real active imagination.

The Sarge has a way of describing things that the finest English teacher in the world, Ms. Roshonda Sue Warren, would say was "interesting and colorful, therefore able to provide a powerful impact."

The Sarge can take you to whole new levels of fear when she calm-as-anything listens to what you have to say, then answers by going, ". . . is that right? Well, let's say you do decide not to exercise the only real option I've given you. I'd have no choice but to slap you so hard that by the time you've stopped rolling, your clothes will be out of style." Try sneering and muttering under your breath to the person who's just broke something down to you like that!

29

I've had to grow up with that kind of thing hanging over my head and know that whether or not you can appreciate it, it's a wise choice to pretend you do. Learning young that you have very little of what we philosophers like to call free will can make your life simple, especially when it comes to something like following rules.

Keeping it real, though, "rules" doesn't come anywhere near to what the Sarge has set up for me.

What she makes for me are called mandates, which is like a rule times ten, or as Darnell Dixon puts it, "Break a rule, lose your allowance; break a mandate, lose your life."

Mandates fit right in with what the Sarge likes basing everything on, something called a military model.

When she first started prepping me to take over her businesses she said, "What better way to run an organization? The U.S. military has had hundreds of years to practice getting things right, and what they do isn't all that much different from what I'm doing in these homes.

"First they have to clothe and feed a large number of people. So do I. And who are these people? For both me and the military they're a large, diverse, often unwilling and ungrateful group who most likely are where they are as a last resort. It's a group of people that needs to have their minds and their time completely occupied or they get antsy. It's a group that finds safety in the group—they may not know it but they neither want nor need individuality.

"Another thing they don't need is that whole warm, touchy-feely nonsense. That brings emotion into it, and emotion is a loss of control. Oh, sure, it's a great feeling to have people looking up and cooing at you, but when you're the one in charge it doesn't work. When push comes to shove you have to be in control at all times. That's something that goes from raising a family to running one of these group homes all the way up to commanding the U.S. Army."

She told me, "I know you're deep into philosophy and love to flip these sayings out all the time so let me run it down to you in a way that you'll get: as a great philosopher once said, 'It is far better to be feared than to be loved.'"

That's another thing that ain't exactly what you're gonna hear on the Parenting Network, but it's worked all these years for the Sarge.

The first mandate I remember her teaching me is the no PDA, or no Public Displays of Affection, mandate.

I was nine or ten years old and the Sarge and Darnell and me had just made our monthly trip to Sleet-Sterling to buy some clothes for her clients. She had an arrangement with Mr. Brandon, who was the manager of the Thrifty Living clothing department, that on the last Wednesday of every month she'd come in and charge a thousand dollars' worth of clothes for the clients. The next day she'd return all the clothes and slip Mr. Brandon a hundred dollars cash money. He worked some kind of magic with the receipts and the Sarge kept the original copies, which she just-like-that turned in to the Department of Social Services. In a week or two she'd get a check in the mail reimbursing her as part of the clients' clothing allowance. When the clients really did need clothes we'd head over to the Goodwill to do their shopping.

But there was a reason for this and it all was for the good of the clients.

"Your average Goodwill clothes are so old they've been washed hundreds of times," the Sarge told me as another take-over-her-business lesson. "That's a virtual guarantee that they're nice and soft and not irritating to people's skin. If the clothes have survived that many washings you know they're high-quality garments. Besides, that designer junk is way overrated, way overpriced and way too flimsy."

She taught me the same lesson with food. We'd buy steaks and lobster once a month and they'd all go right over to the Sarge's place and not to the homes. Then we'd head to Costco or the Warehouse Club and buy a ton of boxes of macaroni and cheese or spaghetti sauce and ramen noodles for the clients. If she was feeling real generous we'd go to the army surplus store and buy a bunch of Meals Ready to Eat. Social Services paid the Sarge back from the steak receipts.

"Steak and lobster are detrimental to their cholesterol levels," she'd told me back when I was young and dumb. "Besides, if those MREs are good enough for the brave, patriotic men and women defending this country, then by God, they're good enough for anyone living in one of my homes."

Those are nothing but Sargeisms, where you have a long list of reasons why something you do is good for someone else, but surprise! surprise! it always seems that you get something even better out of it.

Anyway, on that day I first learned about the no PDA mandate, we were leaving Sleet-Sterling and going out the front door of the mall. I saw something that nearly made me puke out my breakfast right on the floor: slick Darnell Dixon reached his hand out and gave the Sarge a good, long, healthy squeeze on her behind when he opened the door for her!

I was at that stage when you think any kind of touching of someone's private parts is about as disgusting as you can get, but, come on, the Sarge? What kind of sick person would want to touch the Sarge?

Especially on her behind?

The Sarge moved like a Serengeti lioness on the Discovery Channel. In a flash she dropped the bag of flimsy, overpriced, overrated designer clothes she'd bought for herself from Sleet-Sterling and pinned Pimp Daddy Dixon against the window with her left hand around his throat and her right hand balled in a fist, ready to knock him deep into next week. She squeezed his throat so hard that his eyes bugged and the juice from his Jheri Curl dripped like a leaky faucet onto the glass of the window.

"Uh-uh," she said, calm as anything, "you will never show me anything but the utmost of respect anywhere I go. Touch me again like that and once you get out of the hospital you'll be singing the unemployment blues so quick your head will spin. Need I say more?"

Poor Darnell couldn't answer because she was crushing his windpipe and he couldn't nod because she had his head on lockdown on the glass.

She arched that left eyebrow and quietly asked again, "Need I say more?"

Darnell managed to let her know that her message got through by making his eyeballs go from side to side.

She let go of him and he fell to the floor gasping and clutching at his throat.

I was impressed. I'd seen Darnell break three fingers of a man who was just too-too late with his payments on a Friendly Neighbor Loan while singing the "Snap, Crackle, Pop, Rice Krispies" song, I'd seen him beat the mess out of a man who was twice his size, and I'd been in the barbershop and had heard them talking about how he'd stood on the railroad tracks once in the middle of the night and waved some kind of secret Mason lodge hand sign at the engineer and made the man stop the train dead cold to give him a ride to Chicago.

But now I was seeing something else that could be added to the Legend of Darnell Dixon; even after getting totally punked out by the Sarge he picked himself up with massive cool, grabbed the bag of clothes she'd dropped and walked us to the car. If it wasn't for his little coughs and throat-clearing and spitting you never would've known anything had happened.

I think I was the only one who was amazed by what I'd just seen. As we were driving home the Sarge sat as calm as could be in the passenger's seat and dug Darnell's neck skin out from under her fingernails with an untwisted paper clip while calmly talking to me about the importance of the no PDA mandate. As if I needed the picture to be painted any clearer.

· 5 ·

ARCHAEOLOGY TODAY'S PERSON OF THE MILLENNIUM

It caught my eye because it was shaped like Madagascar. I was almost done scraping the loosest of the paint off the living room walls when one of the paint chips flew off in the exact shape of that big island off the coast of Africa. I bent down to pick it up and turned it over in my hands. This was unreal! There was even a old, dried-up, reddish-brown spot right where Antananarivo, the capital, is!

This was definitely a sign. Maybe it wasn't something as deep or obvious a sign as Jesus waving at me out of a freshly fried tortilla, but no doubt, this Madagascar paint chip had "sign" written all over it.

And it was a sign that was meant for me.

I mean how many other Flintstones even knew what Madagascar looked like, much less where its capital is? The mystery was trying to figure out what someone was trying to tell me.

I kept scraping and thinking, thinking and scraping. I took my wallet out and stuck the paint chip in it. Then I took my student planner to write a note to remind myself why I did that.

At Whittier Middle School they give you this spiral student planner notebook at the beginning of every year. I carry it around with me all the time because at the back they've got about thirty lined pages where you don't have to officially put anything. It's like they made a mistake and gave you your own little private section of the book.

At the top of each page they've got the word "Musings," and as a philosopher I like the idea of me sitting around and musing. That sounds a lot better than sitting around staring off into space, and a lot of teachers and other ignorant types confuse the two. I use that section to write down any philosophical things that I might think of.

I've learned that if you don't write down what you're thinking about, no matter how amazing it is you'll forget it. I don't like to brag, but I know I've had a couple of ideas that were so great and shocking that they'd've won the Nobel Peace Prize for Philosophy. The only problem was I didn't write them down and by the time I got home or got out of the shower they were long gone.

I turned to the back of my planner and wrote, "Madagascar paint chip in wallet—DON'T THROW OUT—important sign from someone."

Darnell Dixon stuck his head into the room. "Man, put that notebook down. You ain't getting paid to be no reporter."

I dropped my planner and started back to scraping.

He said, "I can't believe you're still fooling around with that scraper, how many times I got to tell you no one cares? Quit slacking on my time and get busy and lay down that paint, youngblood."

The Sarge used to joke that when it came to getting slum housing up to close-to-livable conditions Darnell was the man.

Cable bill a little too high? Darnell Dixon can hook you up with a pay-one-time satellite that'll get you so many channels you could get last Thursday's high school volley-ball scores from Uzbooboostan if you wanted to.

Electric rates more than what seems fair? Darnell Dixon's a magic man when it comes to making meters turn a whole lot slower.

Short on cash and got some insured property that's just sitting around? Darnell Dixon's started more fires than seven out of ten cigarette lighters.

Want to encourage some low-life tenants to move on? Who you gonna call? Darnell Dixon.

He probably could've been a tough investment banker, too, 'cause even though the Sarge only pays him minimum wage he buys a new one of those triple-white Rivy Dogs of Love every other year. And they want some big cash for those babies.

He's the Sarge's favorite employee, someone who she says "knows how to get results." As part of her plan to leave me the business when she retires she kept sending us out together hoping that some of his tricks of the trade would rub off on me. But Darnell was smarter than that, he knew I was a hopeless case and gave up on me years ago. This is

37

part of the reason he hates my guts so much. He figures I have it made and don't appreciate it. He thinks I'm as soft as you can get. He's never said it to my face but every time he looks at me his eyes spell out P-U-N-K!

In the Sarge's eyes Darnell Dixon is also the lord of all painters, only because the brother can completely paint the inside of a two-story, four-bedroom house in five hours and forty-one minutes, closets, attic and basement included. Of course this doesn't leave much time for cleaning up or prepping or taping or cutting or moving anything out of the way, but oh well.

He's painted over dust balls the size of small watermelons, nails as thick as an elephant's leg and picture hooks big enough to snag and hold one of those nuclear submarines, but the Sarge is more worried about speed than anything else so Darnell is her man. And I'm honored to work with him.

I know that many thousands and thousands of years from now Darnell Dixon will be a true hero to archaeologists, anthropologists and anyone else interested in studying these times. They'll worship him because his painting has single-handedly trapped whole slews of twenty-first century Flint flora and fauna. If there was a magazine called *Archaeology Today* Darnell Dixon would be their Person of the Millennium.

When it comes to laying down the paint, this brother does not play. He's right up there with volcanic ash and the La Brea Tar Pits in the specimen preserving department. Amber and fossilization don't have a thing on him.

He's painted over dozens of species of roaches, spiders, centipedes, birds and even small mammals. It would break a lot of kids' hearts to know it, but half the missing pets in Flint are plastered to the walls of the Sarge's houses after dying horrible, suffocating deaths buried under layers of discontinued Dutch Boy paint just 'cause they weren't fast enough or strong enough to avoid Darnell Dixon and his Roller Brush of Death.

When Darnell finishes a room the walls might be a little lumpy, but you can bet every square inch is slathered with paint, and that's all that the Sarge and the renters seem to care about when I show them the houses.

If they ever start dropping the nukes or weapons of mass destruction I'm heading right over to one of the houses that he painted 'cause with all the paint that covers the walls there's no way in the world that radiation or anthrax could ever get through them.

I finished painting the living room while Darnell finished the kitchen. And the dining room. And three bedrooms. And two hallways.

After I cleaned everything up and changed back into my school clothes it was time for the ride-home inspection.

"Hands," Darnell said as we stood on the front porch.

I showed him both hands, palms up and palms down.

"Shoes," he said.

I leaned against the railing and showed him the bottom of each shoe.

"Turn."

I slowly turned around twice while he made sure no

paint or nastiness was anywhere on me. I felt like I was doing the Hokey Pokey.

He pointed the remote trunk opener at the car, clicked the button and said, "All right, get the sheet."

Darnell calls the sheet his anticootie protector. Anytime me or any other hard leg is going to ride in the car I have to get it out of the trunk. He'll spread and tuck it over the backseat and down into the place where you put your feet. The whole thing takes about five minutes 'cause he checks and double-checks to make sure no part of his Rivy Dog is exposed. After Darnell finishes covering those seats the greatest forensic scientist from the Cold Cases Network wouldn't be able to tell I'd ever been anywhere near the car.

Finally he nodded and I climbed in.

The first time he did this, about four or five years ago, I'd thought it was cool. I mean here I was a little kid and I was getting chauffeured from home to my chores in the backseat of a brand-new Riviera just like I was some kind of millionaire! It didn't take long before I figured out that this was just another way that sour, jealous old men use to humiliate you when you're young and virile.

One time I'd asked Darnell how come I had to ride in the back. He said, "Because you have the wrong anatomy to be sitting in the front seat of Darnell Dixon's Rivy Dog of Love."

I didn't need any more details beyond that. Besides, if I was in the front seat I'd be that much closer to the lame, old-school R&B songs that Darnell always played, tired old folks like the Temptations, the Funkadelics, Marvin Gaye.

That stuff that was so old and played out they didn't even bother to make a video for it.

On the way back to the home I blocked Darnell's music out of my mind and kept wondering why I was getting this sign dealing with Madagascar.

Maybe it was sent to show me that I should keep hope alive, that someday I'd leave Flint and head back to the Motherland.

Maybe it was sent because there was some fine Madagascar sister waiting to help me free Chauncey, be fruitful and multiply.

Maybe the Madagascarinians were in a desperate search for a young king who could give a great shave.

Maybe I'd better quit dreaming and get to thinking about that science fair project. I had to get approval for what I was going to do in less than a month.

Darnell interrupted my thinking. "We gotta roll over onto Fourth Street, I'ma need about three gallons. You'd best make good and sure them lids are sealed tight before you put the paint in the trunk."

Fourth Street is where the Sarge stored the two billion gallons of paint she bought real cheap a long time ago.

And just like that the sign revealed itself! The science fair project was sitting in my wallet sandwiched between Chauncey and my library card and it was shaped just like Madagascar! Madagascar wasn't what it was about, that was just a sign pointing me in the right direction!

What'd I tell you? Philosophical thinking had paid off again! Just that day in biology Mrs. Bohannon was talking about something that I could blow up into a project! I took out my planner and started making one of my Luther T. Farrell patented lists. This was one idea that wasn't getting away.

Between school, homework, laundry, shopping, doing dishes, general watch duties, prepping and painting houses, hauling trash, running the clients to therapy, to classes, and to their doctors' appointments, getting them up, giving them their a.m. meds and shaving them in the morning and bathing them and giving them their p.m. meds and putting them to bed at night, it took every second of the next two weeks to knock out most of the research for my science fair project. All that was left to do now was write it and throw it all together. I could tell when that was finished the three-peat was most likely in the bag.

The only reason I was saying "most likely" was Shayla Patrick, not only the daughter of Flint's biggest undertaker, but also the curse, and the love, of my life.

Last year I had a close call with Shayla and the science fair and I wasn't about to let that happen again. Last year's fair had been full of surprises. When they made the announcements at the assembly the first had been that Bo Travis got third place. Bo is one of those super-quiet and laid-back brothers who never has nothing to say to no one. He works at Halo Burger after school and always wears this black pants and purple shirt uniform. He even wore it in his seventh-grade school pictures, he even wore it when he picked up his award. We all were surprised that he'd done so good. Usually you need some serious cash to put a top project together and Bo was always at his J.O.B. but always seriously broke. Broke with a capital "B."

The second surprise last year was when Shayla got second place and I got first. Even though I'd doubted myself for a little bit after I'd seen her project I guess the judges knew what was what.

She went so deep into hate-eration that she waited three whole days before she got up the nerve to walk up in my face and say, "You know and I know who really should've won first place. I don't know how you did it, but next year I refuse to be cheated out of my gold medal."

Even though I'm in crazy love with the girl all I could say to her was "Is that right? Well, listen here, Morticia, why don't you take some of that dripping bitterness and raging jealousy that are chewing on your heart and have your old man bury them with the next stiff that he gets."

I don't know why, but the only time my mind seems to work when I'm around her is when I'm dishing out disrespect. She showed her beautiful, perfect teeth, growled and stomped off.

If I was gonna win this year's science fair I was gonna have to bring it strong. Shayla Patrick didn't know it then, but her challenge from a year ago had inspired me to greatness and the project that I'd come up with was the bomb!

· 6 ·

MOVING DAY

The next day I stopped by the Sarge's after school. I have to drop by her place every day to get briefed on what was happening with inspections, complaints, visitations and other junk. As soon as I pulled into the driveway I knew something messed up was about to jump off. The Rivy Dog of Love was there and the anticootie sheet was spread and tucked across the backseat. To make things worse, the Happy Neighbor Group Home pickup truck had been pulled out of the garage and was parked next to the Riviera.

Aw, no!

That could only mean that Darnell Dixon had given his main flunky, Little Chicago, a ride over here. And that could only mean that they were about to go and evict someone. And that could only mean that I was going to be doing a cleanup and making a dump run. And that could only mean pain.

This is one of the things that I hate the most about working for the Sarge. There's something that's straight-up terrible about throwing people out of their homes. I mean these rental places may be the Sarge's houses but they're also someone else's homes.

The begging and crying and wailing of freshly out-on-the-street people is always sad, and before you get used to it, it will cost you a bunch of sleep. What's just about as bad, though, is having to haul away what these people leave behind. These things always remind me of what's left over of a nightmare the next morning, all you've got is a bunch of scraps and flashes of memory that only give you a hint of how scared you'd been during the bad dream, and it's even worse because they *are* only scraps and flashes, they let your imagination fill in the blank spaces with a truckload of made-up horror and sadness.

In a cleanup it seems to me that what's left behind is what sticks with you longer than the evicted folks' tears.

There's no way to know what you'll find but it's never going to be something that's gonna pop into your mind later and leave you smiling.

Just a couple of weeks ago I had to go on a dump run and took Sparky with me. Darnell and Little Chicago had already gotten rid of the people and stacked all their stuff on the curb. All me and Sparky had to do was load the garbage in the pickup and take it away. There was so much junk that it looked like we'd have to make three trips to get rid of it all.

Sparky climbed into the bed of the pickup and said, "You hand the stuff up to me, I'll load the truck."

If he hadn'ta come along I'd be doing this all by myself so I didn't see anything wrong with him automatically jumping up to do the easiest part of the work.

I started handing the cardboard boxes to Sparky. One of them seemed extra heavy. I hefted it onto my knee, then slid it onto the rear gate of the pickup. As soon as Sparky picked it up the bottom fell out.

Along with the bent forks and coverless books and ripped-in-half lottery tickets that spilled out was the biggest, baddest, ugliest, nastiest-looking rat that had ever walked the streets of Flint. It tumbled out of the box into the bed of the truck, landing with a smack that sounded like someone had dropped one of those great big Polish sausages on a tile floor.

The rat's tail was as thick as my thumb and as long as my forearm. He looked like he had either been in a fight and got bit or had been chewing at a sore on his back. There was a quarter-size bright pink bare spot there that was soaking wet and oozing neon-green pus along its edges.

If the rat had wanted to kill me and Sparky we were there for the taking because all either one of us could do was hold our breath and stare at him with our mouths and eyes wide open.

The rat looked back at me with black, shiny, marble-sized eyes and shook himself like a wet dog. He jumped off the truck and strolled about two feet past me as calm as anything, then waddled up the front steps onto the porch and back into the house. He was being so cool that I was surprised he didn't slam the door behind him after he got inside.

46

Sparky finally squealed and scrambled backward into the trash that was already in the truck. Then he jumped right out of the pickup's bed onto the street.

I told him, "She must be crazy if she thinks I'm gonna load this mess up."

Sparky was already inside the pickup's cab with the door locked behind him.

By the time I got behind the wheel, he was cranking his window up. I locked my door and said, "I'll tell you what, that's it for me. She's gotta get her exterminator out here before I pick up one more box or bag!"

I started the truck.

Sparky was shaking like a cold Chihuahua. He said, "I thought I was through. Man, that rat was diseased, did you see that thing on his back? Looked like he had lurvy or something."

"Had what?"

"Lurvy, that disease sailors used to get if they didn't have no vitamin C."

"Whatever. But that's one trash pile that won't be seeing Luther T. Farrell until a professional exterminator can give me documented proof that he's killed everything in it. And the Sarge doesn't have all day to get it done, either, I'ma give her two hours or she's gonna have to get someone else to haul that trash. I got other things I can be doing with my time."

Sparky and I had a good old time laughing about the rat and telling each other how we were about to go off on the Sarge. But with every block that we got closer to her place, the laughs and the jokes got fewer and fewer.

47

By the time I pulled into the Sarge's driveway the inside of the truck was dead quiet.

Sparky looked at me and said, "Well, let's get this over with. I wonder what she's gonna say?"

I didn't have to wonder.

When we walked in the Sarge was just hanging up the phone.

She didn't even look at me. She picked up a logbook, started writing in it and said, "I know you couldn't've moved that rubbish that quickly. What's up?"

As a great philosopher, whose name escapes me at the moment, once said, "Fools rush in where wise folks would never stick a toe."

Sparky blurted out, "Mrs. Farrell, you won't believe what happened! I picked up this big heavy box and a rat as big as a rottweiler came rolling out of it! Then he strolled up in the house like he owned the place! He had some kind of skin disease!"

She finally looked up. "And . . ."

Sparky said, "And? Well . . . and . . . and Luther said we wasn't going back out there until you get all of them boxes and junk exterminated. And you gotta get it done quick, Luther says he's only got two hours before he has to take care of some other business."

That's my dog.

I could tell the Sarge liked this. It's not like she smiled or anything, but there was a certain, I don't know, cheerfulness in her usual Billy Goat Gruff voice. She said, "Is that right?"

She tipped her head at me. "Listen. I don't care if you pick up one of those boxes and Smokey the Bear comes strutting out of it."

She looked at her watch. "It's currently fourteen hundred thirty hours. When I drive by there at seventeen hundred hours for inspection I want to let you know that there are two, and only two, outcomes to this little drama that I'd find acceptable.

"The first: I go by there and see a nice clean curb in front of a nice clean house. That I'd find acceptable."

Poor Sparky, he stood there listening and nodding like there really were going to be some choices given here. I took on the right pose for one of these lectures, I kept my eyes on my feet.

The Sarge said, "The second outcome that I can live with is that I drive by there and see that the trash is still on the curb. In that case the next thing I'd better see is signs that a violent confrontation has taken place. And there in the torn, bloodied grass I expect to find your fibula or one of your kidneys or some fragment of your skull covered with giant rat tooth marks, something that shows you put up a struggle of Biblical proportions before you were eaten. That, too, I'd find acceptable. Sad, but acceptable."

The left eyebrow arched. "Need I say more?"

When we got outside Sparky said, "You do know you're on your own, don't you? I mean you do understand where I'm coming from and where I'm going, right? Peace out, baby."

He started walking home.

Just like most times it was me against the world.

That's why I was so unhappy to come up here today and see the Riviera with the anticootie sheet and the pickup truck.

I opened the door to the Sarge's.

Darnell and Little Chicago, or as I call them behind their backs, Satan and Satan Lite, were just getting ready to leave.

Darnell told me, "Forty-three-oh-nine North Street. Give us about a half hour, that crackhead calls herself refusing to leave. It shouldn't take too long to make her see the error of her ways."

Little Chicago did his sick stupid laugh. He said, "Oh yeah, she's gonna see it like she's got fifty-fifty vision!" He's the only person I know who really goes "Tee-hee" when he laughs.

As Darnell walked past I could see he'd put his 9-millimeter pistol in the back of his waistband.

Great.

Ever since that time I had what the Sarge called "an irrational, inappropriate episode of misplaced sensitivity" at one of Darnell's evictions I've been excused from going to them. That was way back when I was a young pup and I cried and actually hit Darnell in the face with a box of Sugar Frosted Flakes when he slapped this six-year-old boy that he was evicting.

I was a kid back then and Darnell let me off on the temporary insanity defense.

He took me aside and told me, "You're messing with my rep, but everyone's entitled to one mistake. Slapping me with Tony the Tiger was yours. I don't care who your momma is, don't make another."

After the Sarge gave me the 4-1-1 on what was going to happen today I went home to take care of my crew, then chilled for another hour just to make sure Darnell and Little Chicago'd had plenty of time to get these folks on North Street out.

As soon as I pulled up on North I knew I hadn't waited long enough. There were two police cars at the curb and a tired, old, leaning-to-one-side, four-door hoopty sitting in the driveway of 4309. I parked behind the back cop car and got out.

The hoopty was running, coughing out thick clouds of smoke and sounding as bad as a big old Harley-Davidson motorcycle. Both windows of the car's back doors had been busted out and had been covered with cut-up black plastic garbage bags that were being kept up by duct tape. The rearview window, over the trunk, was busted out too. They must've run out of duct tape or bags, though, 'cause it wasn't covered. Inside the car I could see the back of someone's head. He was sitting in the rear seat of the hoopty with his chin tucked down into his chest.

The woman who was getting evicted was standing on the porch yelling at two cops. There was a little six- or seven-year-old girl standing next to her. Half of the girl's hair was done up in real neat cornrows with small blue ribbons on the end of each braid. The other half was standing straight up like it'd just been combed out. The woman's right hand squeezed the little girl's shoulder while her left hand pointed and stabbed at the air in front of the cops.

51

She told them, "How you gonna just stand there and let that fool stick a gun in the nose of a fourteen-year-old boy? I wanna press charges."

The little girl was standing stiff as a statue, her eyes were clenched closed and both of her hands were balled up in fists covering her ears. Her mouth was wide open.

One of the cops said, "Look, Ms. Wilson, we checked, Mr. Dixon has a CCW permit and he said your son threatened him. Besides, the witness said Mr. Dixon never pulled his gun. There's nothing we can do."

She screamed, "If he didn't pull the gun out how come my son's nose is bleeding? How'd that happen? You think he bust his own nose up like that? How you gonna let a grown man pistol-whip a boy?"

The cop sighed. "Ma'am, I don't have time for this. You've been legally evicted, and you've got to move on."

The woman yelled, "How's that legal? I know my rights, they didn't give me no sixty days' notice!"

The cop said, "Well, the eviction notice says you were served two months ago."

"The notice is a lie. That crazy dog Darnell Dixon came by two days ago, on Sunday, and told me I had to get out!"

The cop told her, "Not according to the papers he showed us. Now you gotta go."

The woman was probably telling the truth. I'm sure the Sarge had found one of her Friendly Neighbor Loan victims who works at the court to backdate the paperwork. That old Sargeism was right: "Don't ever believe your lying eyes until you see it written on paper."

The woman said, "Where am I supposed to go with no kinda notice?"

The cop said, "I'm sorry but that's not our problem. Are there any other possessions of yours that you need to get out of the house?"

The woman screamed, "I already told you all we have is in the trunk! But you know that's not the point! He hit my son in the face with a loaded gun! What are you gonna do?"

The cop was getting tired of this. "Ma'am, if you don't get in your car and leave, what I'm gonna do is arrest you for trespassing."

The second cop decided they'd do their version of that good-cop, bad-cop thing you see on the Real Life Detective Channel; this version was called bad-cop, bad-cop.

He said, "That vehicle of yours is violating every noise and emission law on the books, the plates have expired and I just *know* you don't have any insurance. But I'ma let you slide. Get in your vehicle right now and leave the area or we'll impound your car, arrest you, and call Social Services to look after your daughter until you can make bail."

Still squeezing the little girl's shoulder like an eagle clutches a rabbit on the Nature Channel, the woman started easing off the porch.

Sound finally came out of the little girl's mouth. She could have been auditioning for *American Superstar*, she let out one note and she was nailing it. It was real high and loud and kind of made the hair on the back of your neck start twitching. She musta had lungs as big as a hot-air balloon.

Once they got down to the sidewalk the woman pimp-slapped the back of the girl's head four or five times and screamed, "Shut up! How's that supposed to help anything?"

The little girl's note died but her mouth stayed open.

The woman snatched open the rear door of the car, shoved the little girl in and slammed the door. Then she opened the driver's door, got in and slammed it, all the while screaming. "All you ever do is think about your own self! You think I want this to happen?" The girl scooted over into the arms of the boy in the backseat.

Then, as if my sleep wasn't going to be shaky enough for that night, the boy looked up and locked his eyes on me through the missing rear window. I was looking dead in the face of the third-place winner of last year's Whittier Middle School science fair, Bo Travis. He'd been crying and there was a double trail of blood running out of his nose and around his lips before it joined up on his chin.

Before I could say or do anything Bo's yelling momma threw the old bucket in reverse, it chugged a couple of times and started backing out of the driveway. As it did, smoke from the exhaust slid over the rusty trunk and into the busted-out rear window.

Bo took his arm from around his sister and flipped me the middle finger.

You could hear Bo's momma's screams from two blocks away. You could hear the car even after she turned right on Black Street.

I went to the pickup and got my broom, the big green plastic garbage can, the aluminum snow shovel I use as a dustpan, a box of plastic garbage bags, some rags, my scrub brushes, the bottle of Pine-Sol and two pairs of gloves, one cloth and the other rubber.

By the time I lugged everything up on the porch Darnell and the cops were joking about something while Little Chicago tee-heed at everything they said.

Darnell was telling the cops, ". . . can't pay the rent but she's down there on Wager every night buying that rock. Here it is five o'clock and she's still laying up in the bed."

He told me, "Start in the kitchen. For as skanky as she was it looks like she didn't leave it too bad."

She didn't leave it bad at all.

The living room was very clean. Except for some notebook papers and blue hair ribbons scattered on the floor, there wasn't a whole bunch of stuff in it. Bo's momma had nailed blankets over the windows like some curtains and the only furniture was a couch and two end tables. Both of the tables had rings of melted candle wax all over their tops. There was one of those metal TV trays sitting across from the couch, probably where they used to keep their TV.

I set my broom on the living room floor and pulled my cleaning equipment into the kitchen. When I went back to get the broom Darnell and Little Chicago had come back in.

Darnell snatched one of the blanket-curtains off the window. A bunch of dust jumped off the blanket and looked like a cloud of swirling, gold-flecked specks when the sun hit it. Darnell threw the blanket down and said, "Them fools had been living up in here with no electricity and no gas for six months. Only reason the pipes didn't freeze and bust back in the winter was because the water'd been cut off in February. She just got it cut back on last week."

"Tee-hee! Tee-hee!"

Now that it was lighter in the living room I could see that both of the melted-wax-topped end tables and the couch were covered with bedsheets. The sheet on the couch was brownish-looking, one of the end table sheets was light blue and the other one was a washed-out sheet that had Masters of the Universe printed all over it.

There were more blue ribbons and a comb and a brush, and a open jar of Dax hair grease and a book called *Tornado* by Betsy Byars sitting on the couch.

Darnell walked over to one of the end tables. "Look at this," he said. "It's a miracle that low-life crackhead didn't burn the place down."

He flicked some of the hardened melted wax off the Masters of the Universe table, then kicked at it. It lifted off like it was light as a feather and flew across the room, bumping into the TV tray and sending it rattling to the floor.

It wasn't a table at all. It was nothing but a big empty box of Charmin toilet paper that had been covered up with a sheet.

"Tee-hee! Tee-hee!"

Little Chicago sent the other end table flying across the room. Another box of Charmin.

He said, "Maybe she wasn't as ghetto as you thought, D, at least she had enough class to buy matching end tables."

Little Chicago hadn't heard anything so funny in his

56

whole life. He sprayed tee-hees out like the roach man sprays Raid.

That was more than enough for me. I could feel another irrational, inappropriate episode creeping up on me.

With Darnell and Little Chicago kicking and tugging and pulling at everything in the living room it looked like a scene from the Animal Planet Channel where a pack of hyenas was slashing at what was left of a zebra.

I got my broom and went back into the kitchen.

Bo's family really was clean and neat. I emptied out the kitchen wastebasket and instead of the usual nastiness that you find, there was only a box of Hamburger Helper, a bunch of those empty little packs of coffee creamer, two empty cans of tuna fish cat food, an empty jar of jelly and an empty jar of peanut butter. And when I say empty I mean empty! The jars and cans looked like they'd been scrubbed out.

Most times cat food is a bad sign, it means there's a nasty litter box somewhere in the house, but it looked like maybe the Bo family's cleanliness even ran down into their pet. There wasn't any cat smell anywhere.

I opened the fridge. The only things in it were a box of baking soda, a bagful of little green apples and one of those plastic zip-up bags that you put six cans of pop in to keep them cool.

If this was a movie on the Fright Network I'd unzip this bag and someone's head or heart would be staring up at me. Or worse, a chopped-off hand would leap out and snatch me by the throat. I walked over to the sink with the bag and slowly undid the zipper. That way if I had to drop it quick I wouldn't spill whatever was inside, I wouldn't destroy any evidence. Once it was unzipped I pulled the top back.

Inside was a small carton of soy milk floating in some water with a bunch of half-melted ice cubes.

This was going to be one of the easiest cleanups ever! The kitchen cupboards didn't have anything in them except a box of cornflakes.

It looked like Bo was getting some perks from his job at Halo Burger. The next drawer had a bunch of red and white Halo Burger napkins, a bunch more of the coffee creamer and some of those little packs of salt and pepper. That was it!

I checked upstairs next. Other than a few loose sheets of paper and some old gym socks the place looked like it had already been prepped. There were no holes in the plaster, no mystery stains on the ceilings, just a few pictures of the space shuttle thumbtacked to one of the bedroom walls.

I saved the bathroom for last, it's always the nastiest, but the only thing in there was another stack of Halo Burger napkins sitting on the toilet.

It was perfect! I wouldn't even have to scrub the floors or the sink or the toilet or anything! This was a record. I'd be in and out in less than an hour!

I'd gone back to the kitchen to get the garbage bag when I saw them. I don't know how I missed them the first time through. The front door and sides of the fridge were plastered with a bunch of those flat little rectangular refrigerator magnets. They all said:

GET WHAT YOU DESERVE!!!
CALL ATTORNEY DONTAY ORLANDO GADDY
FOR THE ORIGINAL PITBULL ACTION!!!
REMEMBER:
BIG OR SMALL
HE WILL SUE 'EM ALL!!!
CALL 1-800-SUE-EM-ALL!!!

On one end of each magnet was a picture of a dog showing his teeth. On the other end was a picture of the American flag.

Maybe there'd be something to smile about when this was done after all. Sparky would get a real kick out of these magnets. I started peeling them off the sides of the fridge and making a stack for my dog. Then I noticed what it was the magnets were keeping up.

It looked like not only being neat ran in Bo's family, being smart did too. The magnets were holding up a bunch of tests and certificates and stuff. All of them had the name KeeKee Wilson neatly printed in the upper right-hand corner. That must be Bo's little sister.

Here were a bunch of tests that she got As and Bs in addition on.

Here were a bunch of tests that she got perfect in spelling on.

Here was a room C Citizen of the Month award.

Here was a Book Worm award saying that she'd read eighteen library books in April.

Here was a report card that was tattooed with nothing but As and Bs.

And here were a bunch of one-page essays she'd got mostly As and B-plusses on.

The one on top was called "Admiration."

She'd written, in penmanship better than mine, spaced out on the paper:

My big brother is 14.
He is smart.
He cares if I'm hungry.
He studies alot and works alot.
I admire him because he is going to fly the space shuddle.
And he keeps his promeses.
And he doesn't pull two hard when he brades my hair.
His name is Bo
And he loves me.

Maybe that would've been too much right there. But I might've been all right if the last four of Dontay Orlando Gaddy's magnets weren't holding up a picture colored with bright crayons. She'd got an A on it, too. Her teacher had written, "Great Work, KeeKee!" It was titled "My Family" and showed three people standing outside of a house with a chimney that had smoke coming out of it. There was a little band of blue sky across the top and a little band of green grass across the bottom. There were five or six "V"s in the empty area under the sky that were supposed to be birds. There was a giant daisy growing next to a little tree. The number on the house was 4309.

She'd drawn a dude and two ladies. The females had skirts that were perfect triangles.

The male was the tallest and was in a burgundy shirt

and black pants. Him and one of the females, who was just a little shorter, were reaching their stick arms to their sides and had joined up the three stick fingers that were on each of their hands. They both had bright Crayola red smiles on their bright Crayola brown faces and two black dots for eyes. The female standing off to the side of these two was about half their size and, maybe KeeKee had run out of black crayon, the little female had a red mouth but didn't have any eyes.

Under the male, KeeKee Wilson had printed "Bo."

Under the tall female holding Bo's hand she'd put "Me."

Under the little eyeless female, KeeKee had printed "Mommy."

I leaned my back against the magnetless fridge and slid down until I was sitting on the kitchen floor.

This was the kind of thing I was talking about, this was the scraps of a nightmare. This was the stuff that you couldn't get used to. This was the kind of thing that would make you want to get that box of cornflakes and put a serious beat-down on Darnell Dixon, Little Chicago and the Sarge.

There's always something desperate and fake when you have to deal with someone who's about to get evicted. They'll say anything to try and get another rent-free week or two. That makes it easy not to listen to what they have to say, 'cause you know there's a pretty good chance they're lying. It's nothing to make your heart hard to that. Even if you feel bad for them odds are they're not doing nothing but playing you, and who wants to get played?

People will throw their babies in your face or have their sick, dying mommas cough on you or they'll tell you the check's in the mail or that the Department of Social Services computer is down or that they've got the inside word on what next Thursday's number is going to be or any of a million other stupid excuses as to why they haven't paid the rent in three months. It gets real easy to let those excuses slide right by you 'cause it's real obvious that they are what Ms. Warren calls rhetoric, or speech designed to influence.

What's hard is a stupid little picture drawn by a little mostly-As student who's got a dope fiend momma. What's hard is knowing that that girl was gonna be living in a busted-up Impala until her momma drags her into some other hole to live. What's hard is wondering, and I know some philosopher somewhere has wondered this and probably figured it out to the day, how much longer that little girl has before she's beaten down so bad that being room C's Citizen of the Month doesn't mean a thing. What's hard is knowing that KeeKee may be six or seven now but that in three or four years she'll be thirty.

That's the kind of thing that'll have you back-slid up against a fridge with a stack of tests and essays and certificates in your hands so heavy that they've pinned your arms to the floor.

That's the kind of thing that has "irrational, inappropriate episode" written all over it.

I don't know how long I'd been sitting on the kitchen floor. I don't know how long Little Chicago had been watching me from the door.

He said, "Darnell, come here," tee-hee, "I think your boy's nutted out again."

Darnell looked in. "Soft little punk."

Tee-hee. "What you gonna do?"

"Nothing, you drive the pickup back and just leave him here. I'll send Patton Turner by later to pick him up."

Little Chicago said, "Who?"

Darnell said, "You know him, Patton Turner. Luther'll be pattin' his feet on the pavement and turnin' the corners to get his soft self home."

It was dark when I started walking. I'd picked up all of KeeKee's tests and her library book and the picture she'd drawn and was carrying them and the fridge magnets in one of the plastic grocery bags. I didn't know what I was going to do with them, but I couldn't leave them. Forty-three-oh-nine North Street had just gone from being KeeKee's home back to being the Sarge's house.

7

SPARKY'S BAD NIGHT

It's funny how when you're young there're some things that old people do that seem to be so tight that you can't wait to do them yourself. Things that make you stay awake the night before they're 'bout to happen 'cause they got you so hyped that you can't even sleep. Things like when I just turned thirteen and the Sarge woke me up to tell me, "I've noticed the rapport you have with the men over at their group home, it seems to me like there's a genuine affection between you and them when you're working over there."

Uh-oh.

Most times if I woke up and found her standing over me my ears would be ringing from one of her "Good morning" pops to the head. Most times her wake-up words were something like "How come you didn't . . ." or "Do you realize what time it is . . ." or worst of all, "There seems to be a little discrepancy in what I requested and what was done."

So these words about me doing a good job at the group home didn't quite feel right.

All I could say was "Really?"

She did that thing that she thinks is a smile and said, "Really. So, even though you're young I've made a decision."

Uh-oh.

"Tomorrow night at eight you and I are going to the Secretary of State's office over on Clio Road. Peter Thompson is going to cut you a driver's license. You're ready to drive the bus."

It wasn't until later that I learned I should always wait for what we philosophers like to call the other shoe to drop. Back at thirteen I was still young and naive. I just about jumped out of bed and said, "I get to drive? Seriously?"

She said, "When have you known me not to be serious?"

This was great! She'd made Darnell Dixon start to teach me how to drive the bus a while ago and he told her, "Are you kidding? That bus costs more than eighty thousand dollars. You gonna let *him* drive it?"

"Just in case," she'd told him. "You never know what tomorrow will bring. Besides, when you start making the payments you can question me about who drives my bus."

I got pretty good at it in a couple of months and now I was actually going to get my learner's permit! I'd probably be the only thirteen-year-old in the universe who would have one.

That's when the questions started creeping in.

I said, "But . . . wait a minute, isn't the Secretary of

State's office closed at eight at night, and don't you have to be sixteen to get a learner's permit?"

She said, "You're right, it is closed at eight, for the general public. I happen to know that since he's the manager of that branch, Mr. Thompson provides twenty-four-hour service for a certain, elite clientele. And as far as having to be sixteen to get a learner's permit, you obviously weren't paying attention, I didn't say a thing about a learner's permit, I told you you were going to be getting a driver's license."

The warning bell went off again, loud.

I said, "But you have to be eighteen to get a driver's license, there's no way I look like—"

She was fed up with me. She said, "Look, just make sure Little Chicago has everybody in bed with their meds by seven-thirty tomorrow. Put on your suit and tie, that'll make you look a little older, you're already freakishly tall for someone your age, you can do this. Once you have the papers saying you're eighteen, that's what you are. I'll get you a birth certificate to confirm your age just in case."

She saw I didn't like the sound of that.

"If it makes you more comfortable why don't you look at it like this, do you have any idea what a difficult period of time the ages of fourteen through seventeen are for most boys? Consider yourself lucky, you'll be zipping right from thirteen years old to eighteen years old, you will officially miss the majority of the turmoil of adolescence and the incumbent nastiness that it inevitably brings."

That was the first shoe of the Sargeism. The second shoe dropped when she said, "I've also decided that starting

Monday you'll take over running the men's home. You'll move over there and be in charge of getting them where they need to be. And don't think you're doing this as a charitable contribution to our business either, I've decided I'll pay you ten dollars an hour for the first forty hours of your work week and, since you'll be putting in considerable time beyond that, you'll get the state mandated time-and-a-half fifteen dollars for everything over forty hours. We'll set up an education fund for you and I'll deposit your wages directly into it so that when it comes time for university you'll be set, you won't be a hostage to a usurious student loan. Taking this over is a big responsibility but I know you can handle it."

It wasn't until later that I found out she'd caught the men's home manager stealing medications and had fired him. That meant she had to come up with someone to run the home pretty quick. Who better than me? Even though I was only thirteen at that time I already was doing most of the work over there and knew the routine, and the men did like me.

But I didn't see it like that back then, I only saw that I was man enough to be driving and in charge of four or five grown folks, plus I'd be moving out of the Sarge's house into a place where I'm the boss!

I'd been so excited I didn't sleep at all that night. I should have known that the next day would be the Day of a Thousand Dropping Second Shoes.

The Secretary of State's office manager, Peter Thompson, turned out to be another victim of the Sarge's Friendly Neighbor Loan Program.

In return for getting a little something knocked off his loan Mr. Thompson was dying to sneak me into the office after hours, photograph me for a driver's license and also order personalized license plates for the bus that said BBY FACE.

"That way it looks like you're known for looking younger than you are, that will deflect a lot of questions," the Sarge told me.

It took about two weeks for the fun of running the home to wear off. Two weeks for all the excitement to turn to dust. Just two little weeks before the thing that I'd been so geeked up about that I couldn't sleep turned into nothing but hard work, boredom and a whole bunch of cartoons and late night TV.

Once you get some years on you and a little experience under your belt it turns out that those things you have great expectations about are just as tired and played out as anything else in your life. I don't know why so many of the fools I go to school with can't wait to get older, it seems like with age fewer and fewer things are exciting. And it seems like the more excited you are about something, the more time you spend dreaming and wondering and fantasizing what it's going to be like, the more disappointing it turns out to be.

Which has got me seriously worried about sex.

But one thing that age and the Sarge have taught me is how to fall into a routine to make things go smoother. I try to make everything predictable and comfortable for the Crew. Change bothers them and makes more work for me so we do everything the same way every day. From shaves to lunches to television, I keep it all smooth and flowing.

Of course these are the life and times of Luther T. Farrell so nothing ever goes all the way smooth, I had just got all the men settled into the dayroom and was starting in on my science fair project again when my worst nightmare happened. One second I was getting research off the Net and the Crew was watching cartoons and the next second Nickelodeon flickered twice during *Little Lulu*, then disappeared, leaving nothing but the blue screen of death. The weatherman had put out severe weather warnings and the winds outside must've really started kicking up.

All six of us in the dayroom groaned.

I turned off the blank-screened TV with the remote and pulled the curtains back to look outside. I could see that the television and computer were probably through for the night.

Branches on trees were slapping at the wind like they were slapping at a million flies. Every once in a while their leaves would zip away as if they'd been shot out of a gun. Someone's garbage can thumped and bumped up the street, a green plastic tumbleweed.

I knew what had happened. That illegal satellite dish that Darnell Dixon had hooked up on the roof was probably blowing around in Detroit by now, being mistaken for a UFO.

Mr. Baker said, "You gotta fix it, Luther, you gotta fix it now."

I had to get control of the situation before Mr. Baker

got anyone else riled up. "All right, gentlemen," I said, "it's story time. Tonight we're going to hear . . ." I walked over to the shelves and looked at the books.

Mr. Baker stuck his arm out like he was directing traffic and shouted, "Amber Brown! Amber Brown! It's been a good while since we've heard Amber Brown."

Mr. Foster rolled his eyes and said, "Not again."

Mr. Baker said, "OK then, how about *Sheep in a Jeep?* What's wrong with that one, Foster, you got a problem with *Sheep in a Jeep?*"

Even though he was locked up here in one of the Sarge's homes, there were times when Mr. Foster's mind was still sharp as a razor blade. He said, "How about as a compromise, Luther, you read that touching story about mad-cow disease down on the farm, *Sheep in a Heap?*"

No one got it but me and I was too worried about Mr. Baker getting hyper to laugh.

Mr. Foster sighed and said, "Pearls before swine, Luther, the story of my life, pearls before swine."

He pulled a book out of the case and said, "How about the white whale, anyone up for the white whale? Besides, Luther, if you read enough of this to us I'm sure most of us could forgo our sleep medication tonight."

"OK," I said, "the white whale it is. Sorry, Mr. Baker, we'll read Amber Brown and *Sheep in a Jeep* again next time."

Mr. Baker said, "Since I can't hear Amber Brown how about letting me go out for a smoke?"

I ignored him and stood in the usual reading place, right in front of the TV, and began reading *Moby Dick*. I mean they'd been conditioned to be entertained looking toward the TV, so who am I to go against that?

The Crew loves hearing me read and why wouldn't they? I throw in a lot of voices and sound effects to help make the stories more interesting, and believe you me, the early parts of *Moby Dick* need a lot of help in keeping anyone's attention.

Ishmael had just let us know who he was when the phone rang.

"Just a minute, fellas. Hello?"

"Luther?" It was Sparky. He sounded like he'd just run five miles. "Have you looked outside, bruh?" I could hear the wind howling behind him.

"Yeah, where you at?"

"I'm on the phone outside Seven-Eleven. It's like a hurricane out here!"

"Then why don't you get inside? Are you coming over?" The 7-Eleven was only a couple of blocks away.

Sparky said, "Uh-uh. I need you to meet me behind Taco Bell."

"You need *what?*"

"Seriously! This is my big chance, baby! Before this night is over I'm going to be calling 1-800-SUE-EM-ALL. I finally got someone to sic the big D.O.G. on." He started barking into the phone.

"Sparky, what are you talking about?"

"I'ma put me a suit in on Taco Bell!"

"Oh, you're gonna do that old I-found-a-rat-in-my-burrito trick?"

Sparky said, "Please, they peeped out that scam a long

71

time ago, they even do autopsies on the rat if you claim that happened. I got the bomb, baby! But I'm gonna need your help."

"Uh-oh."

"Uh-uh, Luther, this is for real. I walked by Taco Bell and all them red tiles are lifting up off the roof and knocking the mess out of everything in the parking lot! One went clean through someone's windshield!"

"Sounds dangerous."

"Which is why you gotta get down here."

I said, "Why would I come out on a night like this to watch some roofing tiles crashing into cars . . ." Then I understood. "Now I get it, you want a witness that you got hit by one of those tiles, right?"

"Something like that, but I need a little more."

"I'm listening."

"I really do need to get hit, and you're the only one I can trust to do it right."

"Aw, no. That ain't happening!"

"Come on, Luther, I already got one of the tiles set to do it. All you gotta do is kinda tap me in the head, then walk me into Taco Bell and have them call an ambulance."

"*What?*"

"Don't worry, bruh, you know when I get paid I'ma break a little something off for you."

"You must be kidding."

"Luther, don't make me beg."

"I can't do it, Sparky. Besides, you're cutting into my science fair project time. Plus I gotta put the Crew to bed, that's going to take at least half an hour."

Sparky said, "If that's the best you can do, half an hour then, behind the Taco Bell."

"Cool."

He said, "I just hope the wind hasn't died down by then, it'll be on you if it has. Your half hour could be costing us a whole lotta benjamins, my brother."

"I'll see you in half an hour, but this better be quick, I'ma just whack you in the head, then I gotta bounce."

Sparky didn't have to worry, by the time I'd settled everyone down and started walking to Taco Bell the wind had even picked up some.

The stop sign on the corner was twisting back and forth in the wind, sounding like a rocket made out of tin cans and duct tape getting ready to blast off. The wind was hot in a way that made you want to close your eyes and tilt your head back and breathe real deep. Or maybe even howl.

Something from the roof of Taco Bell somersaulted through the air, then smashed into the parking lot. Sparky popped out from behind a Dumpster and ran toward me with a tile in his hand.

"Sparky," I yelled, "this is insane, man, let's just go home."

Sparky shook his head and said, "Come on, bruh, hurry up, this ain't real easy for me, you know."

I took the reddish-brown clay roofing tile from him. I was surprised how heavy it was. He leaned toward me, closed his eyes tight and showed his teeth.

"Come on, Luther, quit torturing me," he whined, keeping his teeth clenched. "Do it!"

I shook my head and closed my eyes. I raised the tile about shoulder high, brought it down on his head and felt a little shimmy run up my arm. Sparky was still standing with his eyes squinched shut.

He looked at me. "That's it?" He brought his hand up, rubbed at the spot where I'd hit him and said, "Man, you gotta be kidding, don't forget this thing's supposed to have blowed off a roof, you really gotta knock the snot outta me, bruh."

I dropped the tile. "This ain't me, you gotta get someone else."

Sparky looked hurt. "What? You supposed to be my boy, who else can I trust?"

He picked the tile back up and reached it toward me again. "Remember what we used to say, 'We'll have each other's backs from womb to tomb, you'll be my boy from birth to earth.'"

What could I say? He was right, we had said that. I took the tile again. It must've weighed ten pounds.

The wind was really starting to get serious. The stop sign had stopped shaking and was now whistling and going back and forth like one of those piano metronome things. Two more tiles jumped off the roof and exploded in the parking lot.

"All right, fool, bend your head over."

I closed my eyes, raised the tile over my head and let it drop on Sparky's skull. Again my arm shimmied. When I opened my eyes Sparky was looking at me the way you'd look at a kid who brought home all Ds on his report card.

He said, "Man, all you're doing is giving me a

74

headache! Swing that tile, brother! I bet if I went and got your crusty old mother she wouldn't have no troubles lighting me up."

If only he knew. The Sarge would've paid big cash to take my place right now. Sparky isn't one of her favorite people. She would've hit him so hard it would've knocked his head clean off. I laughed. "Leave my mother out of this."

"Oh! Maybe that's what I gotta do, maybe if I talk about your nasty old momma you'll get mad enough to really crack me with that tile."

Sparky knew I didn't care what he had to say about the Sarge.

"Your momma's so old," he started, "she was the maid of honor at Adam and Eve's wedding!"

He closed his eyes and bent his head over again.

I couldn't help laughing.

He yelled out another stale joke: "Your momma's so ugly, she entered a ugly contest and they told her, 'Sorry, ma'am, no professionals allowed!'"

I laughed again.

Sparky said, "All right then, how about instead of cracking on your momma I talk to you the way she does? Seems to me like that's the only thing that ever gets you mad. Think that might make you smack me with that tile?"

Sparky's left eyebrow arched and he began swiveling his head on his neck the same way the Sarge does when she's about to go off on me. He dropped his voice an octave. "Well, Mr. Luther"—it was scary, he had her down pat—"I know you're so much smarter than everybody else around here, even though it's me that owns two thousand houses around Flint, even though it's me that's got two million dollars cash money in the bank."

He switched from the Sarge's arched eyebrow to the soulfully deep stare. "And I know you're the one that's got all these high-and-mighty plans to be a fool-losopher one day, but the truth is that the best thing that's going to happen to you is that you're gonna be running these houses for me for the rest of your life.

"I know all that, but I still got to insist you get your highly educated, highly motivated self in there and scrape out Mr. Baker's funky drawers again, I can smell the man from outside, or is that too much to ask of a genius-in-training?"

A great philosopher, whose name escapes me at the moment, once said, "The greatest of truths are often said in jest." And even though Sparky was fronting that he was being funny I knew he meant everything he said. There are some things that don't need to be exchanged between friends.

Sparky had crossed the line and he was about to get his wish. I wasn't going to hit him for talking about my momma or for teasing me, but oh yeah, I was going to hit him. I was going to hit him 'cause this felt like a flagrant foul. This felt totally unnecessary. There are things I wouldn't throw in his face, things I wouldn't remind him of, but I guess he didn't feel the same way, so now it was lesson time. Why would someone who was supposed to be your boy try to go off on you where they thought they could hurt you? Besides, I didn't come out of my house on a night like this to be disrespected by my so-called best friend.

Everything moved in slow motion, the way it does when you're about to get in a fight or a car wreck. I raised the tile over my head and this time Sparky's eyes got big instead of shutting. He started to raise his left hand but wasn't quick enough. I snatched my arm down and the tile caught him right above his left ear. This time when it hit, my arm didn't shimmy, it shook. All the way back to my shoulder.

A gusher of thick red blood exploded from a gash on the top of his head and the tile broke clean in half. It seemed like things were going so slow that I even saw a little cloud of reddish-brown dust raise up from where the tile popped him.

Sparky took three steps back, then fell in a pile limp as a towel you just dried off with after a shower. It seemed like all of his bones had been Jell-O-fied.

He moaned, "Oh, no . . . , oh, no . . . ," and propped himself on his left elbow, trying to get back up.

I dropped the half tile I was holding and started over to help him.

A woman's voice came loud and strong, even with the wind pounding on everything around. "Hey," she yelled, "you better leave him alone! We saw you hit him! The cops are on the way!"

I looked over toward the Taco Bell. The manager and two of the kids who worked there were standing in the doorway. She waved a cell phone at me, she'd really called 911!

"Uh-oh, Sparky, quick man, get up! They saw what happened, come on, we gotta get outta here!"

I pulled Sparky to his feet. Blood was running down the left side of his face.

He still hadn't figured out what was going on. "Luther? Bruh?" He kept bringing his hand from the cut down so he could see the blood. "Why'd you hit me like that, man? What'd I ever do to you?"

"Sparky, the Taco Bell folks saw what happened, it's over, we got to move. Besides, you might need to get to the hospital, your head's running like a spigot!"

He finally understood what was going on. I took off toward the alley and he stumbled along just behind, trying to keep up with me.

We were back at the home in two minutes.

I used my key on the back door and guided him down into the basement. I led him right into my bathroom. Blood was coming out of his head real fast.

I knew the Sarge would kill me but the closest thing to stop his bleeding was one of her good white towels. We'd just had a state inspection so the everyday towels were still hidden in the linen closet upstairs.

"Here," I said, and handed him the white towel, "press this on the cut, it'll slow the blood down. I'll go get the keys and drive you to the hospital."

My roommate, Chester X Stockard, looked up from his bed and gasped. That was the most I'd seen him react to anything. Maybe he'd had some bad experience with blood before.

I told him, "It's all right, Mr. X, Sparky had a little accident, I'ma take him to the hospital."

He closed his eyes.

I left Sparky leaning over the tub and ran back upstairs.

As soon as I opened the kitchen door the Sarge was standing at the sink. Sparky's run on bad luck was still going strong, she almost never came over here at night.

She said, "I thought you'd gone to bed."

"Uh, I thought you had too."

She said, "Tomorrow I want to change Mr. Baker's medication, seems to me like he's getting a little too—"

There are some knocks that have bad news written all over them. They're a little too hard or a little too soft, whichever, but you know when that first knuckle hits the wood that whatever's on the other side of the door it ain't someone telling you you hit first prize in the Lotto.

The Sarge looked at the clock in the microwave, then at me. "You expecting someone?"

"Me? No. Uh-uh."

Her eyes stayed on me a second too long as she wiped her hands on the dish towel. I started back down to the basement.

"Hold on," she said. "I got a feeling about this, you follow me."

I jumped when the knock came again.

The Sarge peeked through the peephole, then looked over at me. The muscles in her cheeks squeezed her jaw tight. She opened the door.

"Flint police, ma'am."

"Yes, Officer, how may I help you?"

"Ma'am, sorry to disturb you. We're checking out an assault and attempted robbery that occurred at a fast-food restaurant a few minutes ago."

"An assault?"

"Yes, ma'am, the witnesses said the victim chased after the suspect. We followed a trail of blood to your house. It seems to have disappeared just down there." I saw the beam from the cop's flashlight swing across the yard. "Have you heard or seen anything unusual in the past few minutes?"

"No, Officer, I haven't, but I will keep my eyes open."

The cop acted like he wanted to ask more, but the Sarge was through. He'd get more information from a fire hydrant than from her.

"Thank you, ma'am. Do you mind if we look in your back-yard?"

"Knock yourself out."

Even before she had the door shut I was already slipping downstairs.

"Front and center!"

I went back.

"Assault and attempted robbery?"

"Momma, it wasn't nothing like that."

"Then what was it like?"

"Well, Sparky . . ." I forgot, the Sarge didn't take to nicknames. ". . . Dewey, had this plan to scam Taco Bell's insurance company and so he made me bust him in the head with one of their roof tiles and he started bleeding real bad and I was supposed to take him in so they'd call an am-bulance and then he'd sue them. He was gonna give me some of the money."

She said, "And?"

"And some people at Taco Bell saw me hit him so we had to call it off."

The Sarge rolled her eyes.

"So where is that idiot? He's not getting blood all over my floors, is he?"

"No, ma'am, I got him a . . ." Uh-oh. ". . . a rag before he came in, he's leaning over the tub downstairs."

"Get him."

I walked as slow as I could back down into the basement. If it wasn't for bad luck . . . It's just the way things go in the life and times of Luther T. Farrell that the one time the cops take less than an hour to answer a 911 call it's when they've been called on me.

I couldn't believe my eyes when I got back into the basement. Chester X was out of his bed and was leaning over Sparky washing around the cut on his head with soap and water.

I said, "Mr. X! You gotta get back in bed, I told you he was gonna be cool, just get your sleep."

He mumbled something, then shuffled back to his bed.

I told Sparky, "See what you did? Now he's all riled up and probably won't get back to sleep."

Sparky said, "I didn't do nothing, I just looked up and there he was, 'bout scared me to death."

I told him, "She wants to see you."

"Who?"

"Who you think? Come on upstairs."

He stood up.

"Wait," I told him, "give me that."

I took the Sarge's good towel from him. It was heavy with blood.

"Lean over the tub in case that starts bleeding again."

81

I ran cold water over the towel and poured some liquid detergent onto it before I rubbed the stains. I lifted some of the stinking clothes out of the hamper and put the towel at the bottom. The Sarge would never see it there and I'd wash it when I did the rest of the laundry on Saturday.

I looked under the vanity for something to put on his head. The only thing there was the rag I use to clean the toilets. It was curled around the top of a bottle of Pine-Sol, so stiff and dry that it felt like it had been carved out of gray, petrified wood.

Oh well.

I pulled a couple of the longest hairs off and ran some water on it until it softened up a little.

"Here," I said, "use this instead."

Sparky looked up and took the rag. He pressed it back into the gash in his head.

I checked to see if Chester X was back asleep. Then me and Sparky started upstairs. About halfway up he said, "Man, this cut has really started stinging." He pulled the rag down. "And what's that smell?"

He put the rag to his nose. "Awww, no. No you didn't. You give me a rag that's been soaked in Pine-Sol? You trying to kill me?"

"What?" I said. "It's a disinfectant. Read the bottle, it says 'Kills germs fast.' I'm looking out for you."

"Oh, I guess that stinging is the germs getting killed, huh?"

He pressed the rag back onto his head.

The Sarge was waiting in the kitchen.

Sparky gave her a weak smile.

"So, Dewey, what's the deal with your head?"

"Uh, nothing, Mrs. Farrell, I, uh, kinda walked into a door. But it wasn't one of your doors, and it wasn't your fault, it was all the way my bad."

Uh-oh, I forgot to tell him the Sarge had already shook the truth out of me about what happened.

She just stared at him.

He said, "And besides, even if it was one of your doors I'd never tell anyone that it happened here, I swear I wouldn't. I swear to God."

"A door, huh."

"Yes, ma'am."

"Let me see."

The Sarge pulled the rag away from Sparky's head. The blood was starting to cake up in Sparky's hair and the rag came away making a sound like Velcro.

I gotta give my boy his props, that had to hurt. He squinched one eye shut but he didn't say a word.

The Sarge's expression never changed.

"You gotta go home now. Tell your mother to trot your ignorant, lying little self to the hospital, you're going to need seven or eight stitches to close that. I'd take you myself but, sad to say, I've got a certain minimum intelligence level that I require of people who get in my car, and I don't think the two of you added together can reach it.

"How are you going to fake an injury and set it up right in front of the place you're scamming? I suppose neither one of you could've thought to pop his head somewhere else, then have him stagger into Taco Bell?"

The Sarge laughed and said, "Then to top it off, not

only do you two waste this good wound, after you put on a public display you act like Hansel and Gretel and leave a little trail of blood for the police to follow you back home.

"Dewey, I can't say I don't like your initiative, but in the future, I'd suggest you stay away from any schemes that involve you getting hit in the head. The way I see it, you're only a concussion or two away from checking into one of my homes as a client.

"You"—she looked at me—"get down in that basement and clean up, it'd better look like Mr. Clean's been through there when you're done, if you get my drift.

"You." It was Sparky's turn. "Go home. I feel like I'm losing points off my IQ just from being in the same room as you. Good night, gentlemen."

Ah-ha! There's justice in the world after all! Fifteen minutes ago Sparky'd been panning on me for having to listen to the way the Sarge was in my grill all the time and now that it was his behind in her sights, all of a sudden she wasn't one bit funny.

She waited a second to see if either one of us was foolish enough to say anything, then arched her left eyebrow and left the kitchen.

I opened the back door for Sparky.

He waited until he was outside, looked back into the kitchen to make sure she was gone, then said, "You better check the Sarge, Luther, she ain't got no cause to imply nobody's stupid. My momma didn't raise no fools."

I looked at his head, with the left side swollen twice the size of the right. I caught the odor of Pine-Sol coming off the nasty rag that was at this very moment re-Velcroing it-self to his scalp, and the only thing I could think was that the Sarge was softening up in her old age. Only *implying* that Sparky was stupid could be seen as being downright compassionate.

· 8 ·

SUCKER PATH STROLL

The next week was a real drag for a bunch of reasons. Sparky'd talked himself into believing that he was about to have a stroke and had been blowing off school because he was getting "unexplained" headaches. The state was coming back to reinspect the home and I was so busy trying to get everything straight that I was only on the third item on my science fair project list. To top it all off I'd had KeeKee Wilson's bag of things in my locker waiting to give them back to Bo for more than a week.

Bo'd skipped all his classes since they got evicted and I was kind of glad because seeing him was something that I wasn't trying to do. Having all of KeeKee's papers around was like a bad omen or something but I couldn't just throw them away.

When Bo didn't show up on Friday I asked if anyone knew if he was coming back to school or where he was living now. Someone told me that he'd picked up a second job at Burger King during the day but other than that no one knew nothing. No one knew and no one cared.

Oh well.

When I got home after school I took *Tornado* out of the bag, then threw KeeKee's stuff in the garbage. I mean, I really had tried to get it back to her but finding Bo looked like it just wasn't going to happen. The book had KeeKee's school's name on it so I could drop it off after I picked up the Crew.

In the Whittier Middle School pecking order Bo is kinda off the chart. Me and Sparky and Shayla and Eloise are really at the bottom of the barrel but Bo and a couple of other kids at the school don't even register on the scale. Mostly they're the loners, people like Bo who don't mess with no one and who don't want no one to mess with them.

KeeKee's papers were putting me in what we philosophers call a moral dilemma. On the one hand since I didn't want to see Bo and I had tried to get the papers back to him it was all right for me to throw the papers away. If they were all that important his family would've taken them when they were getting evicted, right?

On the other hand they had to be important to KeeKee. She must've worked real hard on them, even though I'm not hating when I say getting all As in the second grade ain't exactly as tough as winning the Nobel Peace Prize for Rocket Science. But for a little kid you can see how that might seem like a big deal.

The bag with all KeeKee's junk sat in the garbage at the home for about fifteen minutes before I pulled it back out.

When you're looking a real tough philosophical problem like this in the eye there's only one moral thing that you can do: you start making compromises.

I figured the best way I could get these papers to Bo was to go by the Halo Burger on Saginaw Street at night and drop them off real quick. I could walk in all blasé, order me a cheeseburger deluxe, heavy on the olives, a cherry Coke and some fries and after I got my grub I'd tell whoever took my order, "Oh yeah, could you give this bag to Bo Travis." Then I'd jet. That way there wouldn't be any embarrassing scenes with words like "How come your momma threw us out," followed by flying fists.

That night I got the Crew settled down for bed, took KeeKee's bag and headed downtown.

I drove around Halo Burger twice, trying to peek into the kitchen to see if Bo was working, but no luck. Then I saw a bike chained up to the Dumpster out back and was pretty sure it was the one he rode all over Flint.

There weren't any other customers when I got inside, just a real short brother in a purple baseball cap, a purple shirt and black pants wiping down tables.

Even though I knew what I wanted I pretended to look up at the menu, at the same time trying to get a peek in the back to make sure Bo was working.

From studying life I've learned that when you're doing the right thing you get little signs of encouragement some of the time, little things that seem to be saying, "Hey, Luther, you're on the right road, my brother, keep on pushing."

As I waited for someone to come take my order I heard from behind me, "Hey, Luther!"

I turned around.

The little table-wiping dude ran up to me and pushed his face into my chest and wrapped his arms around my waist.

He said, "Pretty darn good to see you again, Luther! How's Mr. Baker doing?"

It was P.D., he used to be one of the clients at the home. About a year and a half ago he went on a special program where some of the clients got to live on their own if they could hold down a real job.

I hugged him back.

I said, "P.D.! When did you start working here?"

He said, "About six months ago. I gotta wipe all the tables and clean off the trash and make sure there ain't no garbage on none of the floors. I'm doing pretty darn good at it too!"

"Yeah, I see, it looks real good in here!"

He said, "Yeah, I been meaning to come on by and visit with you guys again but, man, they keep a brother hopping down here and I'm taking me some classes, too, so I just haven't had the time to do it. How's Mr. Baker doing?"

I said, "That's cool. Mr. Baker's still the same old same old."

P.D. laughed. "Yeah, man, what a guy! Tell him P.D. said hello."

"OK."

He looked over his shoulder and said, "I get in trouble if I stand around talking too much, Luther, this night manager is pretty darn tough."

I told him, "All right then, you better get back to work. Peace."

P.D. turned around to get back at his table.

Then it hit me, this was the little sign that I needed to show I was on the right road!

I said, "P.D., is Bo Travis working tonight?"

He said, "Oh yeah, pretty darn nice guy, that Bo Travis."

"Could you give this to him?" I handed P.D. the bag.

"Sure, Luther, I should've known you two were friends 'cause you're a pretty darn nice guy too."

"Thanks, P.D."

He said, "Wait just a minute, I'll go get him."

I said, "No! That's all right, I'll catch him later. I really gotta bounce."

P.D. said, "Cool, Luther, I'll give it to him right now. Don't you worry, you know if I say I'ma do something I do it."

When I got in my ride and drove by the front of the restaurant I could see Bo standing near the counter looking down into the bag.

That was all I needed, I turned right onto Fourth Street smiling my head off.

Doing the right thing is like that, you get a strong feeling of relief, sort of like a giant rock has been lifted off your back. Or like the dump you take the day after you eat the ten-taco special from Los Aztecos.

I know there's no way I can help most of the folks that are trapped in the Sarge's Evil Empire, but it sure does feel good to help even one.

This is one feeling the Sarge never has to worry about

because she's never done anything decent for anybody. Me and her just look at things different.

But that's cool 'cause one of the things I've learned from studying philosophy and watching Judge Judy is that there are always two sides to every story. Things aren't ever what they seem to be when you first look at them. What's important is that you keep your mind wide open and try to understand what's going on from a lot of different angles. That's what I try to remember every time I talk to the Sarge or think about her or try to understand why she is the way she is.

It finally sunk in that she wasn't like most other moms when I was in the third grade. It was back in the day when me and Sparky still hung with Eloise and Shayla, and I can let you know straight up that we didn't bunch together because we were the siddity committee. Kind of the opposite. We each had something real whack about us that made us stick out as much as it made us stick together.

Sparky was messed up because he never had any money and came from a family with a long tradition of breaking and entering. Eloise was whack because she was smart and didn't try to hide it and didn't mind beating the mess out of anybody, male or female. I was uncool because even the dumbest of my classmates was starting to pick up on the fact that I was a lot more maturer than most anybody else (and maybe because word had leaked out that even back in third grade I had to change the Depends on some of the Crew), and Shayla had a bad rep 'cause not only was she smart, but she lived in a house full of freshly dead corpses.

Me and Sparky and Shayla and Eloise had been on the playground at school when Eloise, just out of the blue, upped and said to me, "My momma said that your momma loans money to people at exorbitant interest rates."

What kind of third grader used words like "interest rates"? Who could ever understand what Eloise was saying half the time? But I could tell from the way she said it that this wasn't something that you'd wanna have your momma called.

I said, "Why are you telling me that? If you wanna borrow some money you've gotta go ask my mother."

She snorted and said, "I don't think so. My momma said the Bible says, 'Neither a borrower nor a lender be.'"

My boy had my back. Sparky said, "Who cares what your momma says?"

Eloise said, "It's obvious that a little gangster wannabe like you wouldn't care, *Dewey*!"

Uh-oh.

I wouldn't've minded watching a good fight but I wanted to see where Eloise was going with this money-borrowing stuff so before Sparky had a chance to go off on her I said, "So what? I know my momma tries to help people out when they're broke. That's why she gives them those Friendly Neighbor Loans."

Eloise laughed right in my face.

Maybe there was going to be a good fight after all. When it came to keeping your respect it didn't matter if Eloise was the toughest fighter in the school, no one laughed in the face of Luther T. Farrell.

Before I fired on her I said, "Why don't you say what you got to say, Eloise?"

She said, "OK, but when you're sitting at home crying your eyes out like a baby later on remember you're the one who asked me to tell you. Friendly Neighbor Loans my foot. My momma says your momma is nothing but a loan shark, and that that hoodlum, Darnell Dixon, shakes people down when they can't pay her back!"

Then, like I was stupid or something, she spelled it out, "L-O-A-N S-H-A-R-K."

It would've been a lot more helpful if instead of spelling it she would've defined it, but whatever this "loan shark" stuff was I knew it wasn't a compliment.

I said, "She is not!"

Eloise said, "She is so!"

"Is not!"

"Is so."

"Uh-uh!"

"Uh-huh!"

I had to get loud on her. I said, "*Uh-uh!*"

She went, "*Uh-huh!*"

I said, "You don't know nothing."

She said, "I know how to speak proper English, and I know a couple of morons when I see them!"

It was a close argument but when me and Sparky were walking home after school he told me I'd won it. He also said if me and her had started fighting he'da pulled her off before she got to whipping me too bad.

We gave each other some dap.

I asked him, "What's a loan shark?"

He said, "I don't know, Luther. But me and Jerome seen this movie called *Jaws* about this thing called a great white shark. You do the math, my brother, sounds to me like she's trying to say your momma is a great big white woman."

"Uh-uh!"

"Uh-huh!"

I couldn't let Eloise get away with saying that, but that was back in the days when I'd still check with the Sarge if I had any questions. If I was going to fight Eloise Exum I wanted to be sure it was gonna be for a good reason. I mean why get beat up for something that wasn't all that bad? From watching the Undersea Life Channel I knew that sharks were at the top of the food chain, so maybe me and Sparky were wrong, maybe Eloise *was* giving the Sarge a compliment.

Back then the Sarge only had two pieces of rental property and was still working at the Buick, so I had to wait for her shift to be over before I could ask her to translate what Eloise Exum had been talking about.

I knew I had to catch her before she went to take her shower and headed off to the U of M—Flint for her classes so at exactly 4:35 I was at the front door waiting.

Before she even had a chance to put her books and her lunch box and her tools down I said, "Momma, what's a loan shark?"

She sat on the bench by the door and pulled her boots off. They always smelled like the factory.

She slid her socks off and started rubbing her feet. The smell of the oil from the shop had even leaked down into her socks. It was such a strong smell that it seemed like when she got to work she might've been taking her boots off and walking around in her stocking feet. I turned my head away, not so much because of the smell, but because I never liked looking at the Sarge's feet, back in the days before her weekly pedicures they always used to be swole up real bad and had knobs and knots and humps and bumps on the toes.

She finally arched her left eyebrow and said, "Why do you want to know about loan sharks?"

I told her, "Someone at school was talking about them."

She said, "Who?"

Luther T. Farrell has never been a snitch. I lied, "I don't know."

She kept rubbing her left foot.

"So," she said, "I'm assuming my name came into the conversation you had with Mr. I Don't Know, correct?"

"Kind of."

"And what did you say when this anonymous person called me a loan shark?"

"I told her you weren't one."

The Sarge said, "And you were right."

She put her socks inside her boots and sighed. "Actually what I do is supply an infusion of capital into a segment of society that is shut out from standard, traditional forms of credit."

So much for translation. They talked so much alike that some of the time I wondered if Eloise Exum wasn't the Sarge's long-lost daughter.

The Sarge had given me that fake smile thing and said,

"OK, maybe I'd agree with Ms. I Don't Know if she said I was a loan barracuda, but 'loan shark' paints much too aggressive and violent a picture for my little enterprise."

I said, "So what are interest rates?"

She stopped rubbing her feet and said, "Eloise Exum."

Before I could even think I said, "How'd you know?"

"She and that little Patrick girl are the only two of your contemporaries intelligent enough to talk about such things, and the Patrick girl has had enough home training to know better than to say something so rude."

"So what are interest rates?"

"Interest rates are the cost of borrowing money, it's what the lender gets for making the loan."

I said, "She used another word talking about the interest rates, ex-something."

The Sarge stood up, stretched and said, "Exorbitant." She laughed. "That's a relative term meaning too high. But the way I look at it no one's putting a gun to anybody's head to make them borrow my money and they know the rates going in, so *caveat emptor.*"

French. Ever since she started taking it at the U of M the Sarge liked showing off by dropping one or two French words into her conversation.

I said, "And what if someone borrows the money but can't pay the loan back, what does Darnell Dixon do?"

The Sarge said, "Look, you tell Ms. Exum if she's got anything to say about my business she should call on me, otherwise tell her I'd appreciate it if she'd quit confusing you.

"All you need to know is that you're going to be taken care of in the future. Beyond that everything is a bunch of rah-rah."

A bunch of rah-rah. As I drove back after giving Bo the papers I thought about that long-ago conversation and I knew that that's what the Sarge would call me stressing out over a second grader's junk.

Moods are funny things. One second I was feeling good knowing that KeeKee was about to get her papers back, and before I could even drive home I'd started thinking about the Sarge and was depressed.

I parked in the driveway, popped in a Busta Rhymes CD and just sat musing.

She just didn't understand me. She just didn't want to understand me.

It wasn't even a month ago that I got up enough nerve to tell her that I was thinking about quitting working at the home and was probably gonna get a job at Mickey D's. That would give me a lot more time to nail this science fair project and get her off my back. I wasn't sure how she was going to react so I told her in my room in front of Chester X. He was all null and void but at least he was some kind of witness.

She said, "You'd think I'd remember, I just made another deposit last week, but what's your education fund up to now? I think the balance was somewhere around ninety thousand dollars."

I said, "Ninety-two thousand, five hundred and ninety dollars since last week."

She went, "Hmm, do you think McDonald's is going to allow you to salt away that kind of funding? You're willing to scuttle your plans for university to work for a clown?"

"Well, it's a start . . ."

She smiled and said, "Exactly. It's a start down the sucker path. Those are distractions and pitfalls specifically made to snare the unenlightened, the uninformed, the unimaginative. Follow that way if you must, but I think your genetic makeup is probably leading you in a different direction.

"I know what so many of your peers' parents tell them, I know the company line where all African American parents are supposed to sit our sons and daughters on our knees, look them deep in the eye and say, 'Life is unfair, you're a young black person, life is going to be especially unfair to you. For you to do half as well as a white child you'll have to be twice as good.' Right? Have you ever heard any such words cross my lips?"

She'd told me a lot, but never anything like that.

"And the reason you haven't is because I can't think of a more hateful or hurtful thing to tell a child. How's that supposed to prepare anybody for life? The way I look at it, that's the equivalent of me being your coach and telling you at the beginning of a race, 'All right, champ, here's the strategy: you train three times as hard as all the other runners, then run four times as fast and if you're really, really lucky and the judges are feeling particularly generous that day they might give you fourth place.' "

Sometimes it's not even worth arguing something, especially when you were hearing it for the thousandth time.

She was like that battery bunny on TV, she was gonna keep going on and on and on. . . .

She said, "How's that supposed to be anything but an incentive to fail? What human being, I don't care how old you are, can't see that there's no way you can win that race? What human being, I don't care how old, can't see that that is a race you have no business even running? That is something you've lost even before you began. That, my boy, is the path set aside for the sucker."

I wanted to argue with her but what was the point?

She said, "I see either a look of disbelief or befuddlement in your eyes, so let me explain it to you again for the hundredth time."

I knew what was coming, the sad and touching story of a young girl trying to find herself in the big city.

The Sarge said, "Before you were born, right after I got my degree in teaching, I got a job in New York City at this chichi all-girls' school right in Manhattan. The people were paying twenty-five thousand dollars a year to send their kids to this school, not for room and board, mind you, twenty-five Gs for the tuition alone. Way more than my salary. Mostly the little brats were the kids of *Fortune* 500 execs, actors, politicians.

"So I'm interning under a teacher and she's doing an art appreciation class and starts to talk about Pablo Picasso and it turns out that two of the little girls in the class have genuine Picassos hanging on the walls at home. One had two Rembrandts. Not copies. Originals. The real deal.

"I went home that day to my fifth-floor cold-water walk-up, looked at what I had hanging on my wall, a black velvet painting of Martin Luther King and John Fitzgerald Kennedy walking hand in hand with Jesus, and I asked myself, 'What's wrong with this picture?' And I wasn't referring to the rather obvious deficiencies in my taste at the time.

"I asked myself how many generations down the line it would be before any relative of mine would have anything anywhere near fine, original art hanging from the walls of their home. I asked myself how many years it would take me to amass enough wealth so that a school I could afford to send my future kids to would have Jessye Norman sing at their eighth-grade graduation. On a teacher's salary I knew it would take me five or six lifetimes to get enough cash to afford a school where we could get James Brown to come in and scream 'I Feel Good' one time."

She kept going and I kept pretending I was listening.

"I asked myself what these little *Fortune* 500 kids had done to deserve so much when my future kids were obviously going to be starting with so little.

"Were they unusually talented or intelligent?

"If so, it was only because any modicum of talent or intelligence they'd shown at an early age had been nurtured and cultivated with the best tutoring and training that money could buy.

"I asked myself if they'd been blessed or preordained to be where they were.

"I realized the only reason it seemed as though they were was because they'd been taught to fervently believe that that was the case. And like I've told you many times before, believing in yourself is half the battle. And like I've told you even more times than that, the other half of the battle is money.

"So during my year at that school my dreams of changing the world through teaching began falling apart just as inexorably and just as irreversibly as the paint on JFK's face began flaking away off that black velvet painting.

"I asked myself what I'd have to do to be able to send my child, or make it possible for my child to send his child, to a school like that one. I knew none of those kids' parents had started right out of school teaching, or working at Wal-Mart, or working in the Buick. Most of them had their money left to them or they'd lucked up and had hit it big with their own businesses where someone had greased the skids for them. They knew that daily nine-to-five action is purely for the sucker.

"And since I knew no one was going to give me anything, the best way I could get a little start-up capital was to come back to Flint, get hired in skilled trades at the Buick, work double shifts and any other overtime I could pick up and start saving money. I knew the only way my pocket was ever going to have any real weight was to set up my own business, to make the system work for me and follow the same rules they follow."

I knew we were getting near the halfway point of the Sarge's speech.

"And believe me, young man, they do follow a whole different set of rules. They milk the system for everything it's worth, and I'm trying my best to do the same thing. I'm milking any- and everything that moves. If it's got nipples, I'm going to milk it."

What kid wants to hear their mother talking about nipples?

She started in with the soulfully deep stare. "Look, I know that may seem harsh, but if you want to learn by experience, go ahead. If you want to go work somewhere other than here you keep in mind that a fast-food worker is three times more likely to be injured on the job than a construction worker and four times more likely to be killed on the job than a cop. Sounds like pure sucker path action to me.

"In the end know that the only thing that's going to earn you the kind of cash, the kind of respect and the kind of life that you can leave to your kids is this business. So when it comes to you working at McDonald's, you tell old Ronald he's going to have to find some other young black child to grind up in his McJob. That's not for you.

"You're too young to remember, but I promised you, right after your father died, that I wasn't falling for the okeydoke anymore, I promised you and myself that just like every big-time exec out there I was going to take care of me and mine first. That's the way of the world, young man, and the quicker you learn it the better off you'll be."

She was wrong. And I was going to prove it to her.

PIT PUPPY CHARMS

"Hello?"

"What's up, Luther?"

"Sparky! Where you been? I was starting to think you'd crawled off somewhere and died."

"Naw, man, everything's tight. I just been off by myself thinking."

I asked, "You still getting those mystery headaches?"

"Naw, man, they went away right after the doc took them stitches out. Peep this, even though hanging with you has been the death of my social life it has done one good thing, it's got me thinking philosophically."

"Oh yeah? How's that?"

"Well, you know how you keep saying that everything happens for a reason and that some of the time it seems like life is trying to send a message to you?"

"Yeah."

"Well, I been getting that feeling too, it seems like life or something's trying real hard to get a message through to me."

"Yeah, it's probably a lawyer from Taco Bell trying to tell you to stay off their property. But that's not the kind of message I've been talking about."

"See? See what I mean? That's one of the main reasons no one can't stand you. I'm being real here, bruh. I really think I need to check out all these signs I been getting."

"OK, so who're these signs from and what're they telling you?"

"On Saturday morning I was waiting for the eight-fifteen bus to go to the fire station and it was right on time!"

"It probably wasn't, that was probably the seven-thirty bus being forty-five minutes late."

"Are you gonna let me finish?"

"Sorry. Go 'head."

"Like I said, the bus was on time and whose face do you think was all over the side of it?"

"Whose?"

"My boy, Dontay Gaddy!"

"So?"

"Hold on. Then I'm sitting on the bus and got my head-phones on listening to 93.7 and who you think the first commercial I hear is from?"

"Let me guess, Mr. 1-800-SUE-EM-ALL."

"You know it, the big D.O.G. hisself. Then to top it off, when I get to the fire station I'm fixing to cut the lawn but Sergeant Forde calls me back in to play one more game of Ping-Pong. So I'm schooling the old man and talking and he starts telling me about his cousin's best friend's auntie that sued Bishop Airport for depressurizing her cat on a flight to Cleveland, and guess who her lawyer was?"

"Hmmm, Dontay Gaddy."

Sparky seemed surprised. "What? Did I already tell you about this?"

"Naw, Sparky, just get to the point."

"The point is that Sergeant Forde starts telling me how straight-up real this Dontay Gaddy dude is. He says that as soon as his cousin's best friend's auntie got in the office Dontay told her to call him by his first name, and even though my boy is just about a billionaire, Sergeant Forde said he'll see anybody for half a hour for free and let you know if you got a case. And what's the bomb is"—Sparky started whispering—"according to Dontay Gaddy, *every fool and his momma's got a case!*"

"So the message you've been getting is to go see this lawyer and get you your free half hour, right?"

"See? It's so plain that even you picked up on it!"

"But who you gonna sue?"

"That's the thing, Luther, I don't know. I figure if I talk to Dontay Gaddy he can give me a little professional guidance as to who it is what needs to be sued."

"And you want me to come with you."

"You know I'd appreciate a ride, my brother, and you know I can't depend on those MTA buses. My appointment is tomorrow right after school so I can't take a chance on being late. Besides, maybe Dontay will have the hookup for you, too."

"Yeah, like I need the Sarge to hear I went to some

nickel-slick lawyer's office. My picture would be on every milk carton in America five minutes after she found out. But I'll take you, I'll have Little Chicago pick up the Crew and watch them for a while. I got the feeling you meeting Dontay Gaddy might be pretty interesting."

"Peace out, baby."

"Peace."

As soon as me and Sparky walked into Dontay Orlando Gaddy's office I could tell that even though the Sarge would have hated his guts, she'd've also had much respect for this man. She'd say that he was someone who knew how to work it. He was like a male version of the Sarge, he was milking everything and anything that moved. Shoot, Dontay Gaddy's reception room was so hype that you could see that this brother could get milk from something that didn't even have nipples on it!

And his receptionists!

They were such hotties that if they'da took off those five-hundred-dollar dresses they were wearing and started running around in a bikini top and some thongs you'da swore you walked into the middle of a 50 Cent video!

Sparky went up to the one at the desk and said, "Excuse me, my name's Sparky and I got a three-thirty appointment to see the D.O.G."

"Just a moment, sir, I'll announce you to Mr. Gaddy." Her voice was just as smooth as the rest of her.

She pressed a button on a control board that looked like it came straight out of the Science Fiction Network and said, "Excuse me, Mr. Gaddy, your three-thirty appointment, Mr. Sparky, is here."

A familiar voice came out of the control board. "Wonderful! Wonderful! Let Mr. Sparky know I've really been looking forward to meeting him and please show him in, Ms. Havens."

She got up and said, "This way, gentlemen."

We followed her down a long hall full of pictures of Dontay Gaddy with a bunch of celebrities. Yeah, in some of them it looked like he'd snuck up behind the celebrity and told someone to real quick take the picture, but in a whole lot of them he was actually shaking the famous person's hand.

As we got closer to his door the pictures stopped being of famous people and started looking like they were of regular Flint folks. They were all smiling and shaking hands with Dontay Orlando Gaddy and holding up giant checks.

The receptionist knocked on this big wood door, waited a second then walked us into the baddest office I'd ever seen.

At the far end of the office was a desk the size of a king-size bed and walking from behind it with his hand stuck out wearing the same serious expression he'd made famous on TV was the D.O.G. himself! And let me tell you, the brother was G'd up!

His suit was another Versace, this one pale blue. He had a thick gold and diamond Rolex on his wrist and was wearing some pale blue Ferragamos that matched the suit.

He grabbed my hand with his right hand and squeezed my wrist with his left. He looked real hard into my eyes and said, "Mr. Sparky, I'm so glad you could make time in your busy schedule to come see me."

I said, "No, sir, I'm Luther T. Farrell. He's Sparky."

Dontay Gaddy kept shaking my hand. He repeated my name, "Mr. Farrell." He sounded so serious that it seemed like he was getting ready to recite the Pledge of Allegiance or something. Instead he said, "It's a pleasure to meet you."

He let go of my hand and grabbed Sparky's and gave him the same two-handed squeeze and stare. "Mr. Sparky," he said, slowly shaking his head up and down, looking so serious that you'da thought he was your doctor getting ready to ask if you had a favorite color in coffins.

He said, "Thank you for coming today."

Sparky was grinning like a fool. "Oh, snap, Mr. Gaddy, thank you for seeing me!"

"Uh-uh, you hold right there, my young brother. My momma named me Dontay, and that's what I want you to call me. From this moment on we're a team, and whoever heard of teammates calling each other Mr. or Sir or"—he pointed at a diploma hanging behind his desk that had "honorary PhD" written on it—"or even Doctor? That's not the kind of team I'd ever want to be a part of."

Sparky said, "Me neither! So you can call me Sparky!"

If that confused Dontay Gaddy you'da never known it.

He kept looking in Sparky's eyes and said, "Sparky."

I got a chill running up my back when he looked over at me with that same creepy soulful and deep stare that the Sarge does and said, "Luther. Gentlemen, please be seated."

Me and Sparky sat in these two bad leather chairs that

felt like they kind of reached up and eased you down into them. We looked at each other and grinned. Sparky's hand was doing the same thing mine was, rubbing back and forth across the arm of the chair. The leather was so smooth and soft that it felt like you were sticking your hand into a pot of warm butter.

Our boy Dontay sat on the edge of his desk, just like he does in his commercials, crossed his arms and said, "Now, what do we have to do to help each other out, gentlemen? Who has left you aggrieved, and what can I do to make you feel better?"

Sparky said, "I just came in here today to check you out and get my free half hour, Dontay. I wanted to run some things by you and see what you thought."

Dontay said, "Just a minute, Sparky."

He walked around to the back of his desk and sat in his chair. He opened a drawer and pulled out this big timer with bright red numbers lit up across it. He pressed something on the back of the timer and the numbers 30:00 came up.

He said, "Sparky, for the next half hour I'm yours." He tapped the side of his head and said, "And when I say I'm yours, I don't mean just my mind, either, I mean my heart is yours too." He slapped his hand on his chest twice.

He said, "Now tell my mind what it is you need my heart to feel. Normally my fee is eight hundred dollars an hour but in the spirit of the team I'm going to give you four hundred free dollars' worth of my mind"—he tapped his temple again—"my heart"—he smacked his chest twice—"and my time." He tapped the top of the timer and the red numbers began counting down from 30:00, 29:59 . . . 29:58 . . . 29:57 . . .

Dontay said, "You may be asking, 'Why is this brother willing to dedicate himself to us so quickly?' And that's a good question, I'm glad you asked it."

I thought, "Huh?"

But Dontay was on a roll. He said, "I'm willing to do it just so you can see how seriously I want to guide you to what you deserve, it's just so I can show you how badly I want to lead this team."

He leaned back in his chair and said, "Now enlighten me."

Sparky didn't want to waste a second. He started by telling the D.O.G. about his bad night at the Taco Bell.

Dontay Gaddy slapped the desk and said, "Brilliant, absolutely brilliant! A little weak in the execution but conceptually inspired!"

Sparky could tell these were encouraging words and started spilling his heart, telling about that sergeant's cousin's brother's nephew and the cat that got blowed up on the way to Cleveland and a thousand other stupid schemes that he had. Dontay Gaddy sat there looking like he was listening to Jesse Jackson instead of my boy Sparky.

I started checking out Dontay's office. Either he'd spent a lot of time in Kenya or he was wearing out the Africana section at Value City. There were enough spears and shields and masks on the walls to get a good Zulu nation uprising going. And a lot more pictures of Dontay and other famous people.

Sparky was going on and on. I checked the timer to see

how much of the D.O.G.'s four hundred dollars he'd used, it was at 22:52. Then, with Sparky jaw-jacking at the speed of light and Dontay Gaddy nodding and going "Uh-huh" and "Really?" and "That's scandalous," every few seconds and my eyes right on the timer, the bright red numbers jumped from 22:17 to 12:17!

I couldn't believe it! I kept my eyes on the timer.

There must've been some kind of foot pedal or remote to it 'cause the next time Dontay leaned forward to slap the desk and say, "Oh, I wish you'd've called me earlier, you shouldn't've let them get away with that!" the numbers dropped from eleven minutes and forty-one seconds to five minutes and forty-one seconds. I'd heard of time flying, but this was crazy!

The D.O.G. leaned forward again and the timer lost another four minutes, leaving Sparky with a little less than a minute to go.

Dontay said, "Sparky, this has been fascinating. Your heart is in the right place, but it looks like we're just about out of time."

Sparky looked at the timer and got his confused look on again. "But . . ." He looked from the D.O.G. to me to the timer. "Oh, snap, I could swear I only started talking a minute ago! But anyway, Dontay, what do you think? Where do you think I'd have the best luck putting a suit in on someone?"

The timer hit four zeroes and Dontay got up and walked around the desk. "Sparky," he said, "I'm going to give careful consideration and due deliberation to that query, but in the meantime I want you to ask yourself, and I hope that you delve deeply within before you answer, who is it that has caused you the most harm? What uncaring, callous, wealthy miscreant has exposed you to some type of imminent peril? Who is it that has put you in a position that a fair mind would call untenable?"

You gotta give Dontay Orlando Gaddy credit, even though he sounded like he'd spent five years in Jackson Prison memorizing the dictionary, he could tell all this was going miles over Sparky's head so as he walked us toward the door of his office he switched gears. "In other words, my brother, who you know with a cold heart and a good insurance policy who it'd be worth the team's while to take to court?"

Sparky was taking Dontay's advice to heart, I could tell by the crazy look on his face that he was delving deep within himself to find an answer. As he walked us down the hall Dontay pointed to the pictures of him and the regular Flint folks and said, "Call me optimistic, call me unrealistic, call me a fool for the little people if you must, Sparky, but I believe that one day your picture is destined to be hanging from this very wall." Dontay smacked his palm on an empty spot amongst all the pictures.

Sparky said, "I don't mind, Dontay, you can put my picture up if you want. The way I see it you're the captain of the team and anything you want goes."

Dontay said, "Oh no, Sparky, you've got to earn your way up here. Every citizen in each of these pictures is a true American hero, every one of them is one of the common folk who let me lead their team and let me work to get them what they deserved. To get up on this wall you've got to come out on top of a lawsuit winning at least half a million dollars! Call me a dreamer, Sparky"—Dontay slapped the empty spot again—"but I see your likeness right here, and sooner rather than later!"

Sparky seemed desperate. "But how'm I gonna do that? I'm ready to take one for the team, D.O.G., all you gotta do is tell me how!"

Dontay said, "Be observant, Sparky, opportunities are everywhere. For example, do you own your own home?"

"Uh-uh, I live out in Stonegate Meadows with my momma."

The D.O.G. said, "Well, there you go, in a complex that large there must be all kinds of attractively dangerous situations. You must be able to find something."

Sparky said, "I'm trying, Dontay, I just can't seem to—"

Dontay stopped walking and put both of his hands around Sparky's head like one of those preachers on the Healing Network.

He said, "Sparky! The good Lord has blessed you with a great imagination, now all you are required to do is to use it! Listen to what that imagination is trying to tell you! Don't you hear it, don't you hear what it's saying?"

Sparky said, "You got your hands over my ears, D.O.G., I can't hear much of nothing."

Dontay said, "It's in your head, young brother, it's that same great inspiration that had you laid out in front of that fast-food joint, it's calling, Sparky, and what it's saying is, 'Ask not for whom the Taco Bell tolls, it tolls for thee!'"

It was like Sparky could actually hear the ringing. He said, "How about if I was taking the trash out one day and got bit by a giant rat with skin disease?"

Dontay let go of Sparky's head and said, "Why, that would be utterly unconscionable and negligent on your landlord's part!"

Sparky said, "Dang, I didn't think that would work, but that's all I could come up with that quick."

Dontay said, "No, no, no, my brother, that would be something that we could use. I like it, think of it, not only attacked by a rat, but a rat with viscous eruptions all over its skin! It almost brings tears to my eyes to think of the emotional turmoil you'd undergo wondering if you, too, would be coming down with some dreaded dermal disease! The only problem I can visualize in that scenario is that although it would be good if you were able to present at the hospital with a horrible wound, it would be a couple of hundred thousand times better if you presented there with both the wound and the vermin that inflicted this trauma upon you."

Dontay saw that he needed to downshift gears again.

"Catch the rat after it bites you and you'll see a whole bunch more benjamins."

Sparky smiled. "Dontay, you take care of your end of the teamwork and let the brother take care of his."

Sparky slapped his hand against the empty spot on the half-a-million-dollar wall. "Only thing is when you snap my picture we gotta make sure my good side is showing!"

Dontay Gaddy laughed. "Sparky, I think all you've got

are good sides. I'm looking forward to quarterbacking this team to the Super Bowl of Litigation! And when I make that final pass into the end zone guess who's going to be there to catch it?"

Sparky said, "Me?"

Dontay said, "Oh yeah, baby. I want you to go home and start practicing your celebration dance."

He put his serious look back on, gave us both the double handshake and the deep look into our eyes, and told the gorgeous receptionist, "Ms. Havens, please make certain brother Sparky and brother Luther receive our calendar, and if we have any more of those fridge magnets see that they get a couple. And to show them how much we want them on the team, I'm waiving all charges for today. I should be paying these young men for the great ideas they have and the suffering they've been through."

Ms. Havens sounded like she was reading from a script. "But, Mr. Gaddy, that's over four hundred doll—"

Dontay Gaddy raised his hand and said, "I know, but I got a feeling about this. Like I said, no charge today."

When we got outside Sparky was pumped. He said, "Next stop, Wager Avenue, home of Marcel Marx."

"What's going on there?"

"Marcel's momma kicked him out so he's apartmentally challenged and is squatting in this abandoned crib over there."

When we pulled up on Wager I should've known, the Sarge used to own the house that Marcel Marx was living in. She'd let it go back for taxes 'cause it had been so run-down that not even Darnell Dixon could bring it back to life. It wasn't even worth having Darnell burn it down for the insurance.

Every door and window was covered with plywood, there were Condemned signs and a spiderweb of yellow police tape all over what was left of the front porch.

I followed Sparky around to the backyard. The back door was a big sheet of plywood on hinges with a round hole about halfway up. Coming out of the bottom of the door was one of those thick orange extension cords, running down the steps and under some leaves toward the house next door.

I said, "What's up, Sparky? This looks like a dope crib."

"I thought you knew Marcel was booming, but don't worry, that's not what we're here for."

I said, "Uh-uh, don't put *me* in this, what are *you* here for?"

Sparky banged on the plywood. It sounded like a eight-hundred-pound bear with asthma started wheezing and growling and snarling on the other side of the door. I jumped off the porch.

Sparky said, "Now, that's what I'm here for."

An eye came to the hole in the plywood.

Someone said, "What you need?"

Sparky said, "Marcel, it's me, Sparky."

The voice came out of the hole. "Who you with?"

"My boy, Luther T. Farrell."

"Who?"

"You remember him; Dr. Depends." Sparky looked at me. "Sorry, Luther."

Your words cannot harm me, my mind is like a shield of steel.

Marcel said, "Oh yeah, hold on, let me chain Poofy up."

It sounded like enough metal was being moved around inside the house to build a bridge.

The plywood door came open and Marcel Marx said, "Come on. Hurry up."

Sometimes being stupid is like falling down a flight of stairs: once you trip on that first step there's not a whole lot you can do to stop from going down, down, down. I followed Sparky in.

The plywood door closed behind us and Marcel threw five or six locks and bars.

The house smelled like Poofy hadn't been out in a couple of months. The inside was lit up by a couple of candles and with all the nasty fumes from the dog in the air it seemed like the crib could blow up at any minute. I started breathing out of my mouth.

That orange extension cord from next door was attached to a little black-and-white TV that had sheets of aluminum foil hanging off the antennaes, it was on channel 12 and hard man Marcel Marx was watching *Little House on the Prairie*.

I kind of sniggled.

Marcel said, "What you laughing at, punk? You ever watched it? The cable man's supposed to be coming out sometime today between four in the morning and midnight, until then that's the only channel that TV will get. Besides, once you watch *Little House* for a while you see what a straight-up wholesome show with a lot of good family values it is. Besides, who you to be laughing at any-one, shouldn't you be changing some grown man's diapers?"

Sparky said, "Whatever. Marcel, we gotta take care of a little business."

Marcel said, "When you start getting high, Sparky?"

Sparky said, "I don't, man, I need something else from you."

Marcel waved his arm around the room and said, "Welcome to Marcel's House of the Deep Discount, you know I'ma cut you a deal, bruh, what you need?"

I looked around the dark room. There were televisions and radios and cameras and boxes of CDs and VCRs and car stereos and cell phones and about twenty different kinds of guns lined up against the walls.

"Naw, Marcel," Sparky said, "I'm not looking to buy nothing, I'm here about Poofy."

"You got someone wants to fight him?"

"Not really," Sparky said, "I'm gonna sue Stonegate Meadows and I need to get bit."

Marcel and I both said, "You need what?"

"Seriously, dog, I need a straight-up bite, and I heard you got the gamest pit bull in Flint so I figured who else to do it."

Marcel looked at Sparky to see if he was for real. He said, "You know I'm running a business here, baby, I'm just like the bus company, we don't do free rides! I'ma have to charge you, Poofy's had a lot of expensive training, I can't let him bite no one for free."

I said, "Sparky, look at the size of that dog, how's that supposed to look like a rat bite?"

118

I pointed over to the far corner of the room. Poofy was there with a chain around his neck thick enough to pull down the Statue of Liberty. The other end of the chain was wrapped around a big block Chevrolet 454 engine.

The dog was sitting there just about perfectly still except he was shaking and trembling like he was a nervous wreck. His two little beady eyes were locked on Marcel Marx.

I guess Sparky hadn't noticed the dog. He looked in the corner and said, "Aw, snap!"

Poofy looked exactly like a snub-nosed crocodile. His head was about two feet wide and his little eyes looked like they were sitting right on top. Even with just the light from the candles and the gray glow of the black-and-white TV you could see the scars and cuts all over his face. His left ear was completely gone.

Marcel laughed. "Yeah, I think I can let him bite you for a percentage of what you get when you sue, 'cause I can just about guarantee once the judge sees what Poofy does to you you'll be getting paid big-time! Check this out."

Marcel picked up a piece of two-by-four and said, "Poofy!"

The dog jumped to attention. A high-pitched whine came from his lizard head.

Marcel threw the block of wood toward the dog and said, "Hit it, boy!"

The dog's mouth came open and he caught the middle of the piece of wood. There was a terrible splintering crack and the piece of wood blew up into a million toothpicks.

Sparky said, "You know what? I'ma have to pass on that,

Marcel. All I want is a bite, I'm not trying to get nothing amputated off of me. Thanks, bruh, but it looks like I gotta do something else."

Marcel said, "Hold on, dog. I might be able to help you out. Poofy's got a couple of puppies that can give you a rat-size bite."

Sparky said, "Oh yeah?"

Marcel opened a door that led into the kitchen and came back with two little pit bulls in his hands. The puppies saw us and started that high-pitched whining and snapping like they were ready to give Sparky what he wanted.

Marcel said, "I'm not gonna have to charge you as much for one of these to bite you, Sparky, we can go with a flat rate instead of a contingency fee, but I do have to warn you about something."

Sparky said, "What?"

"Well, they'll bite you if I tell 'em to, but we might have a problem 'cause some of the time these bad boys want to lock up."

I said, "What's lock up mean?"

"They might bite you and not let go for a while."

Sparky looked at the snarling pups and said, "So how long's a while?"

Marcel said, "You never can tell, it might be fifteen seconds, it might be twenty minutes, but it might be three or four hours."

Sparky said, "Four hours? And what am I supposed to do, walk around wearing these dogs like a charm bracelet for four hours? You know what, Marcel, I really do appreciate you giving me a discount on the puppy bite, I really do, but I seriously gotta pass on that, too."

I was proud of my boy, he said, "Come on, Luther, let's bounce. I'ma fall back on plan B."

When we got back in the ride he said, "So have you rented out that crib yet?"

"Which one?"

"Come on, Luther, you heard what Dontay said, we gotta work this as a team now, you know what I'm talking about."

"Maybe I wasn't paying enough attention, Sparky, but I don't know which house you mean."

"The one on Rankin with that sick rat."

I laughed. "So you're going back over there and what, smear some baloney on your arm so the rat comes out and bites you? Then I guess you'll tell him you'll break a little somethin' off for him if he comes down to the courthouse with you."

"Listen, bruh, like I told Dontay, you let Jesse rob this train, just answer the question, have you rented it out yet?"

"Uh-uh."

"Then can you get me the key?"

"What you need the key for?"

"Look, Luther, can you get me the key?"

"You know I can."

"That's all I need to know. Don't worry, bruh, like I said before, when I get paid I'ma break a little something off for you."

"I'll get you the key. Then count me out, I don't want anything to do with this. But one thing you do have to do for me, you better not let anything happen to that house. The Sarge's already inspected it and I gotta show it to some tenants on Wednesday."

The phone rang a few days later.

"Hello?"

"What's up, Luther?"

"Not a thing, Sparky, what's up with you?"

"Slow motion, bruh, but I did it."

"Did what?"

"Uh-uh, I'll be by in a minute, this is something you gotta see to believe. You know how I've eaten a lot of them MREs and ramen noodles at your crib for all these years?"

"Yeah."

"Well, I'ma let you in on a little somethin'-somethin' and after I do we're gonna be dead even, bruh. After this you might even owe me."

"Yeah?"

"Yeah! In a minute."

A little later I answered the front door for Sparky. He was huffing and puffing and there was something that looked like one of those end tables from Bo's momma's house with a red and white tablecloth over it on the porch behind him.

I said, "What's this?"

He said, "Come on out, you're not gonna believe what I got to show you. But one thing that you are gonna believe is that your boy is looking out for you."

You know how it goes, whenever he has a chance to trip

down the stairway of stupidity Luther T. Farrell will be there, tumbling big-time. I closed the door behind me.

Sparky said, "Squat down real close to it."

Why not?

"Closer."

When my face was a couple of inches away from the cloth Sparky said, "My brother, our days of financial worry are officially *finito*, after this we are outta Flint forever!"

He snatched the tablecloth away.

The first thing my brain picked up on was that Sparky had put a cage on the porch. I noticed the shiny, skinny silver bars running up and down. Then I noticed something gray and gigantic and furry with a wide-open, very pink, very wet mouth, with very long, very yellow teeth coming at me like a fist.

Adrenaline is cool. I saw this show on the Medical Mysteries Channel about how you've got this gland that triggers something in you called fight or flight response, something that decides in a snap if you're gonna stay and battle whatever it is that has scared you or if you're gonna try to get on out of there.

What I got must've been a supersized shot of adrenaline 'cause it triggered both fight and flight in me at the same time: I was gonna get out of there, and I was gonna fight anything that tried to stop me from getting out of there.

By the time the rat's teeth rammed into the bars of the cage I was on the other side of the porch scratching at the wall and making twitchity little animal sounds.

Sparky said, "Oh, snap! Check it out, he almost went and bent the bars of the cage!"

It's kind of hard to get your dignity back when you've been mewling in a ball like a sackful of day-old kittens, but I pulled it off.

I stood up and said, "Are you out of your mind?" My legs were like Jell-O.

It was that same nasty rat, and it didn't seem like he'd missed a meal since the house on Rankin was cleaned out. The only thing was that his lurvy was getting worse, it had gone from being the size of a quarter to being the size of a dollar bill and was running down off his back all the way onto his left rear leg. The dirty gray of his fur and the bright pink of his skin and the neon green of his infection made a real nasty combination. The two Designer Dudes on Home and Garden TV would've called it "a most unfortunate color palette from which to choose."

The rat made another charge at the bars of the cage. This time when he hit, a spray of slobber came out of his mouth. The whole cage jerked two feet across the porch, making a sound like someone was trying to slide an upside-down shopping cart across a concrete floor.

With all this drama the rat had knocked himself a little woozy, he must've took a pretty good pop ramming himself into those bars and he stood there shaking his head a couple of times after that last hit.

Sparky said, "It's all right, he's like a bird in a cartoon, once you get the cloth over the cage he chills right out."

Sparky tossed the tablecloth back over the cage just as the rat made his third charge.

Sparky said, "What'd I tell you and Dontay? He takes care of his end of the teamwork and I'll take care of mine!"

I still hadn't caught my breath. "Where'd you get that?"

"I called the Humane Society all naive and innocent and told them there was a racoon in my backyard that looked like he'd been eating Cool Whip. They were out there in a hour with one of them live-catch cages.

"I borrowed the cage, mixed up some Spam and Velveeta and molasses and stuck it on a piece of bread and set the cage and the bait in your momma's house and the next day, instant rat! My only problem now is trying to decide what I'm gonna wear when the D.O.G. puts my picture up on that wall!"

I said, "I don't know, Sparky, I think you got problems that run a whole lot deeper than that."

Sparky said, "Now, I know I don't have the rep for being real smart, but I really don't think that's the tone of voice you should be using on your partner who's about to be a half-a-millionaire, is it?"

I told him, "All I know is you better get that rat outta here before the Sarge or Darnell or Little Chicago sees it. What if it got loose in the group home?"

Sparky said, "That's the other thing we gotta talk about, Luther. I already took care of my part of the teamwork"— he pointed at the tablecloth-covered cage—"and Dontay's about to take care of his, so the way I see it there's only one person who's kinda letting the team down."

I couldn't help laughing.

Sparky said, "I know you said you didn't want nothing to do with this, but I thought it'd only be right if I gave you a shot at getting bit too. We could say you tried to stick the garbage in the Dumpster and the rat bit you then I went heroic and tried to pull him off of you and he got me."

I laughed even harder.

Sparky said, "I thought you might react like that, but you'll feel different when Dontay slides us a check for a couple hundred Gs."

I said, "Sparky, I'm serious, what if the Sarge comes up here and wants to see what you've got under that tablecloth? You gotta get that outta here."

He said, "That's cool, but I'm not leaving till you help me."

"Help you how?"

"It's like this, Luther, I tried to let that rat bite me, but every time I stuck my hand in the cage and he'd charge at me I just couldn't hold still. Something kept making me pull my hand out at the last second."

I said, "It was probably the last brain cell you got that's still working."

He said, "Go ahead and hate, but I just couldn't do it. So what I need is for you to blindfold me and hold my arm still when I put my hand in the cage."

He stuck his hand in his back pocket and pulled out an old do-rag and reached it toward me.

I laughed again.

He said, "Go ahead and laugh, but I'm not leaving till you do it. Womb to tomb, baby, birth to earth."

I saw the serious look in his eyes and knew he meant it. I thought about it for a second. What are friends for if they can't help you make your dream come true?

I snatched the do-rag away and said, "Take it in the backyard."

He smiled and said, "I knew I could count on you, bruh!"

Holding your blindfolded best friend's hand in a cage so he can get bit by a diseased rat isn't as easy to do as it sounds.

Sparky washed his hand real good with antibacterial soap and we tried three times to hold it still enough for the rat to get at it. But every time Sparky heard the rat scrambling across the cage to bite him he got strength like Superman on 'roids and yelled and jerked away.

Sparky took the do-rag off his eyes and looked real discouraged.

The only thing I could think of saying to help was "Why don't I go in the house and get some cotton balls? We can stick them in your ears and that way when the rat comes busting across the cage to bite you you won't be able to hear him, and if you can't hear him you won't know when to pull your hand away."

Sparky thought for a second, then said, "You know what, Luther? I'ma have to do a reality check on my life. If the only way to get out of Flint is by me getting bit by a rat with lurvy something ain't right. Something's missing."

I said, "How come you always wanting to get out of Flint so bad? You're doing better here than a whole lot of folks."

Sparky said, "Look who's talking, Mr. I'm Gonna Move and Go to Harvard One Day. You know just like I do, Flint's nothing but the *Titanic*, Luther. And the last life preservers they handed out were jobs in the factories back in 1976. Nowadays if you don't go to college you might as well start practicing saying 'Would you like to Jumbo-Size that Chuckie meal?' Back in the day my uncle said even if you didn't finish high school you could still get a job on the line in the factory and make enough cash to buy a new Buick every four years or buy a house or buy some clothes from Hudson's or afford cable TV or a legal satellite. You can't do that now, you can't do nothing with *two* minimum-wage jobs now. Seems like the only way to get paid is being a stickup kid, booming weed or suing someone."

He said, "That's how come I can't see why you keep knocking your hookup with the Sarge. Ninety-nine percent of the fools in Flint would kill to be set up like that."

I said, "Well, that's exactly what they'd be, fools."

It was like I said before, you don't know what someone else's life is like until you live it. Here me and Sparky were thinking that each other had it made in the shade, me because his momma didn't put any kind of pressure on anything he wanted to do, and him because he thought the Sarge and her cash was where it was at.

Sparky sighed and said, "Could you take me back over to Rankin Street? I think the best thing I can do is give this rat a ride back to his house, let him go and think of something else to do."

To cheer Sparky up I thought of a couple of other ways for the rat to bite him but his mind was made up, it was like something had died in him. My boy was seeing things in a different way.

· 10 ·

THE QUEST FOR THE ASHY BROWN KNEECAP

She did it again.

Right in the middle of fifth period Shayla "I See Dead People" Patrick and Eloise Exum started whispering back and forth and I know they were talking about me. Shayla looked so beautiful it made me want to cry. She was leaning in toward Eloise and looking deep into her eyes and smiling and nodding her head, the same way I imagined her doing it with me. They were having a great time.

Finally I had enough, I just wanted to get into their conversation somehow so I whispered to Eloise, nice as anything, "Why don't you two shut up?"

Eloise laughed and, right after she rolled them, Shayla's beautiful brown eyes filled with disgust.

I kept thinking about that tired old song that Darnell plays in his Rivy Dog all the time, "It's a thin line between love and hate."

But what really got me was that Shayla completely ignored me after that.

By the time I picked up my crew at the rehab center later that day and got them to the home I was totally depressed.

I took out my spiral notebook, opened it to the back and started musing.

Who knows why we remember what we remember and forget what we forget? You'd think certain things would be so important that you'd remember every little detail of what happened for the rest of your life, and other things would be so trifling that you'd have to fight to remember what they were a couple of seconds after you saw them.

But nope, your brain is on a mission of its own, it picks and chooses what it thinks is important. It doesn't care what you or the world or anyone else thinks, it's got a plan of what it's going to keep and what it's going to let go of and once your brain has decided to follow that plan, all the concentrating in the world won't make you remember something and all the wishing and hoping and praying in the world won't make you forget something else.

Take that pain, Shayla Patrick, for example. My brain has decided our first meeting is something that I'll be sitting in an old folks' home thinking about when I'm forty or fifty years old.

It was the first day of kindergarten and the Sarge had taken me to school. I remember being scared as soon as she opened the classroom door. The room was stinking from panic and was filled with a bunch of kids my age, crying their souls out and hanging on to their parents' legs.

One kid was screaming, "Momma, please let me come home, I'll be good. Please! Please! Please!"

Another kid was whispering, "Goodbye, Mommy. Am I being brave? You are gonna come get me, aren't you? OK? Is this being brave?"

But the scariest of them all was the little boy whose mother had already left. This kid was standing by himself in the middle of the floor with his eyes rolled back in his head and his teeth chattering and his knees actually banging together. If this was on the Cartoon Network his knees would've been making that funny, hollow clop-clop-clop sound, but in real life the noise that was coming from him was more of a squish-squish-squish sound, all because brother-man had gone and peed his pants.

I can look back now and understand that it wasn't weakness or softness that had me being scared, now I know there was some good, sound science behind my fear. We just learned about minnows and largemouth bass in Mrs. Bohannon's science class. She told us that if a bass grabs a minnow and takes a bite out of it some kind of special red-alert chemical is released from the hurt minnow. You can't see it and I don't think even chemistry geniuses have figured out what it is, but it lets any other minnows within four or five miles know that one of their partners just had a bunch of violence perpetrated on him.

All the minnows in the lake would suddenly start screaming and shaking and looking nervous while they headed for the nearest rock or lily pad or whatever to hide under. The bluegills and the salmon and the perch and the carp would go about their business like nothing had happened, but in the minnow community it was like the Department of Homeland Security had jacked the alert level all the way up to Tabasco-sauce red.

That was what my six-year-old mind was picking up in that kindergarten class. Sure, the adults were calm and smiling but why wouldn't they be? They were like the perch and everything else in the pond that wasn't a minnow, everything was cool as far as they could see. But us kids were the minnows, we knew what the real deal was: somewhere in that school one of our own peeps had psychologically spilled blood and was chemically letting the rest of us know to get on up and get on out. We didn't know anything about hiding under a rock, but we had the screaming and shaking and looking nervous part down pat.

I remember reaching up to grab the Sarge's hand.

She yanked me toward where the teacher sat.

"Hello, young man, and what might your name be?"

Panic was rising up in me quicker than the interest rates on one of the Sarge's Friendly Neighbor Loans.

The Sarge did the finger curl on me and brought me back to reality.

The teacher said, "Don't be afraid, honey, what's your name?"

"Luther T. Farrell, ma'am."

The teacher looked down on a list and said, "Good, I'll talk to your mother and you can go over to the sandbox."

I gripped the Sarge's hand harder until her left eyebrow arched. I knew what I had to do, I mean sure, the air might be filled with chemicals warning me about some invisible danger, but the Sarge was real and visible and there right

132

then and apt to strike without giving *any* kind of a warning. I let go of her hand as quick as I could.

I looked over to where the teacher was pointing. In the corner of the room there was a plastic shell-shaped swimming pool filled with sand and toys but my eyes slid right over them because standing right in the middle of the pool was something that took my kindergarten-baby breath away.

Your memory can play such dirty tricks on you. I know it's not possible, but I'd swear on a stack of Bibles that there were flowers floating in the air all around the little girl who was standing there in the shell. And a couple of angels blowing wind at her out of their mouths making her long, thick black hair dance away from her face.

But my lying memory didn't let it go at that, I can remember there was one of those banners or ribbon things like what beauty pageant women wear around the little girl, but instead of saying Miss Flint or Miss Personality this one had a message that I knew came direct from heaven. It wrapped around her like a snake and had written on it, "Finally! After all these years of practice, I got it perfect!"

I remember thinking it was like the sweetest butter and the brownest brown sugar and the darkest chocolate in the world had melted together, then had had life breathed into them by a kind and loving God.

There's that old philosophical story about how billions and billions of years ago there weren't any individual people, how each person was actually two souls that had been stuck together. And how someone had done something to seriously piss off a god or head honcho or whoever was in charge and how as a punishment that god had divided everybody's souls in half and scattered them all over the world.

In this story you can only know real, true, slam-dunk love when you hook up with that other half of your soul, that's the only time and way you can ever be really whole. It almost never happens but when it does it's supposed to be something you instantly know and deeply feel. That was what was happening with me and the little girl in the shell.

I hate to tie everything to the shows I watch in the day-room but if it fits, what the hey? This longing to get whole again is like what I saw a little while back on the Animal Channel. It was a show about a professor who was doing some kind of research with chimpanzees at a school. She'd raised this one chimp named Mikey for five years before she got a promotion and had to move across the country to her new job. She felt really bad about leaving this little monkey 'cause they'd got real close to each other. She said she thought about Mikey lots of times over the next years.

Fifteen years after she last saw Mikey she got another job back at her old school. When she got there she asked if anyone remembered a chimp named Mikey and what had happened to him. They told her that him and some of the other chimps had been "retired" and were living in a special place at the school. Sort of like a chimpanzee old folks' home.

She said she felt really funny about going to see him. She said she didn't know if he'd even remember her, fifteen human years is about a thousand chimp years. She went anyway.

As soon as she walked into the Old Chimps' Home there was a horrifying shriek like they'd accidentally slammed someone's fingers in a door. Then one of the old gray chimps came tearing across the grass screaming like he was on fire.

He threw himself into the scientist's arms, almost knocking her down. He wrapped his arms around her shoulders, buried his face in her neck and screamed and screamed. The woman just held him, opened her mouth, blinked a couple of times, then cried. It was the saddest thing I'd ever seen. It was even sadder because the woman hadn't known until that second that Mikey had spent his whole life grieving for her.

That's what getting back together with the other half of your soul is supposed to feel like. That's what I felt when I saw Shayla Patrick standing among the sand and toys.

All I could do was look at this divine little hunk of humanity and think, "Oh. Oh my."

The sounds of all the other kindergartners in emotional agony faded away and this beautiful little girl was the only thing I could see, hear or feel. I don't know how long I sat in that sandbox pretending I was playing with the plastic steam shovel while I was really checking her out, but when I looked up the Sarge was gone; the little knee-knocker, who turned out to be my boy Sparky, had been taken out of his puddle and cleaned up; and the teacher was leading everyone who wasn't too traumatized in a song and dance called "Do Your Ears Hang Low?"

The only reason I noticed was because Shayla knew the words and, just like someone had cranked up a CD in heaven, was singing them from where we were in the sand-box. I did all the motions to the song and moved my lips like I knew what I was singing, but my eyes never left her. Then she smiled at me during one of the funniest parts of the song. I quit the fake motions and the fake lip-syncing and found out the meaning of the word "dumbstruck."

I couldn't decide what the most beautiful thing about her was, but I sure wished I had the chance to check her out over and over until I could.

Was it her smile? Even the raggedy little gum holes where her front teeth used to be were beautiful.

Was it her eyes? I hadn't seen eyes as brown and sparkly since I first set sight on my old dog Bone Thug.

Was it her hair? Her hair looked alive.

It was in a million thick dreadlocks and long and about six different shades of shiny, shiny black. It reminded me of waves or dancing, or what the electricity running from a fully juiced nuclear power plant would look like if you peeled away the insulation and rubber that coated the wires leading away from it.

Right after nap time, Shayla got up and was standing next to my mat sharpening a colored pencil. I can see it so clear that I still remember what color the pencil was, it was aquamarine. And I still get kind of tight in my throat whenever I see an aquamarine-colored pencil.

I couldn't help myself, I kissed my fingertips, then touched her knee. When I pulled my hand away I'd left three little wet fingerprints. I brought those three fingers to my lips again and I know the teacher thought I was napping but for real I was out cold! My brain had gone and decided this was enough joy for one day and I don't remember any-thing after that.

The Sarge claims to remember lots more. She says that was the cause of my first visit to the principal's office. The school had a zero tolerance of sexual harassment or un-wanted physical contact and I still own the record for being suspended quicker than any other student in the history of Stewart Elementary School: three hours into my first day of kindergarten.

Darnell Dixon remembers it in a different way too. He's always bringing it up and telling people about "the time this fool got busted trying to feel up the undertaker's daughter."

But see what I mean? If it really did happen that way it seems like that's what would be burned in my memory. It seems like I'd've remembered being dragged down to the principal's office and publicly humiliated, but no, all I re-member is how my lips tingled when I kissed my fingertips after touching Shayla Patrick's ashy little knee.

Maybe philosophers have it all wrong, maybe *that's* what life is all about. Maybe that's why your brain won't let go of moments like that, maybe what we're all looking for is to get back to that moment of perfect happiness. Maybe life's not so complicated after all, maybe it's just about try-ing to get back to that ashy brown kneecap one more time.

Now here it was nine years later and I was still gonna have a rough night over something as stupid as Shayla ig-noring me today after I asked her to quiet down.

· 11 ·

MR. GOODBYE CRUEL WORLD

One of the best ways to get problems with your woman off your mind is to bury yourself in your work. I wasn't about to let Shayla's ignoring me get me down so after I put time in on my project I started early on my chores around the home.

Chester X was upstairs watching TV so after I made my bed I started on his.

I tucked in his bottom sheet, then pulled the bed away from the wall to get at the other side. A corner of something plastic caught my eye. At first I thought it was part of the wrapping that had covered the mattress when it was new. I tugged at the plastic and instead of coming off in my fingers it got bigger. I pulled the bed farther away from the wall to see what was going on.

Oooh! When the Sarge saw this, blood was gonna flow! Some fool had gone and cut a three-inch slit in the mattress and stuffed something inside of it. I tugged at the plastic and finally out popped a Baggie full of pills, Demerol and Valium mostly, a good forty or fifty of them.

Why in the world would Darnell Dixon hide these down here? I'd always thought there was some kind of monkey business going on with him and Dr. Mark and the meds, but this just didn't make any sense. Why would he hide something way down here in the basement in Chester X's bed? This seemed too strange for even him to do.

Then I got it. These pills weren't Darnell's, they were Chester X's, and I knew what he was up to. He was saving his nightly meds to take all at once and bump himself off!

Aw, no! That ain't happening!

There was no way in the world he was going to kill himself while I was in charge.

I've watched the Coroner Channel enough to know how a medication overdose would look. Even though Chester X was in his eighties and that usually means you're carrying a sign on you that says "natural causes" when you die, I know some coroner might want to open him up exactly because he *was* eighty and looked like he was somewhere around fifty.

With my luck it'd be a slow day at the morgue and someone would say, "Quincy, let's see what kept this old fart ticking." Then it'd be me and the cops and a rubber hose in a dark room talking about my medication procedures. Not to mention what the Sarge would do to me if her "special," no-next-of-kin, five-A client committed suicide.

This was one of those things that not even Dr. Mark would be able to make go away. I know it's Sarge-think, but

Chester X Stockard was messing with my livelihood. Not to mention my life.

I finished making the bed to give myself a chance to cool down. I finally felt like I wasn't going to blow up and stuffed the Baggie of pills into my pocket and went to the dayroom to bust Mr. Goodbye Cruel World.

He was on the couch in front of the TV, looking like he was half watching cartoons and half nodding off. But I knew the real deal, I knew there was a whole lot more cartoon watching than nodding off going on. From the number of pills I had in the Baggie in my pocket I knew he hadn't taken any kind of a downer for a good two or three weeks. Chester X was fronting this whole confused, doped-up old man bit.

I had to smile. He'd fooled me and the Sarge, something that wasn't easy to do. You had to give the man his props, he was good. But I guess you don't get to be over eighty years old with five "A"s after your name unless you got some pretty good game.

"Chester X Stockard," I said, plopping down on the couch next to him, "how's everything going today?"

The sly dog let a little trail of drool come out of his mouth while he mumbled something. Most times I would've wiped the slob away, but since this was probably all part of an act, I let his lip leak.

I asked him, "What's Johnny Bravo up to today?"

He grunted, gave a weak smile and pointed one of his shaking, twisted fingers at the television. Stupid me, all of a sudden I started feeling guilty. This didn't feel right. I was acting just like the Sarge. I hate it when she knows I've done something wrong and also knows I don't know she knows. She plays this same little cat-and-mouse game with me, and now I could see that being on either end of it made me feel terrible.

I had to give the man more respect than this. I took a piece of paper towel and wiped his chin and said, "Look what I found in your mattress, Mr. Stockard."

Chester X Stockard looked at the Baggie I was holding, then raised his gray-ringed eyeballs to my face. He let out a low sigh, like he'd been holding his breath for a long, long time. He sagged into the couch and for the first time since he'd come here it was easy to believe he was a tired little old man.

"What's this all about? When and why were you planning on checking out?"

It was scary. He unsagged and his eyes all of a sudden got sharp. He looked around the room and whispered, "Where's the Sarge?"

Wait a minute. "How'd you know I call her . . ." Then I remembered, I'd done a lot of talking to him and in front of him when I thought he was doped up. I answered, "She's over at city hall with Darnell."

"Let's go down to our room and talk."

"*Our* room?"

"Your room. Quit fussing and help me up. I been hoping to have a heart-to-heart talk with you and now seems to be the time."

I pulled him up and we headed downstairs. As I walked behind him I started thinking about what was going on. This new look of spark and spunk in Chester X Stockard's

141

eyes was starting to make me very nervous. Then I knew why.

It's one thing to share your room with someone who's just hanging around waiting to croak. The worst that can come of that is waking up and finding out your roommate is suddenly a lot chillier and less talkative than he was when he went to sleep. After that happens with three or four roommates it's pretty easy to handle. What's harder to deal with is trying to remember everything you said in front of someone that you were pretty sure was unconscious.

You say a lot of things you wouldn't ordinarily say if you knew someone was listening—not only listening, but understanding. And I have this bad habit of talking to the Crew no matter how out of it or unconscious they are. I mean why not? An unconscious person is always a real good listener and never gives you any kind of backtalk. Besides, even though some of the Crew might seem like they don't understand everything that's going on around them, you never know, maybe they like being talked to like human beings instead of just clients.

Then, like I could hear a roof tile from Taco Bell whistling through the air, somersaulting end over end in slow motion, BLAM! it hit me and nearly knocked me down!

Aw, no, this couldn't be happening!

Not only would you *say* a lot of things out loud to yourself that you wouldn't ordinarily say if you knew you had conscious company, late at night in the dark you also might *do* a lot of things to yourself you wouldn't ordinarily do!

Especially if you're the owner of the world's oldest condom.

Especially if you've got a very active imagination.

Especially if your English teacher is as fly as Ms. Warren!

Aw, no! That couldn't've happened!

Suddenly, having a heart-to-heart talk with Chester X Stockard didn't seem like such a smart thing to do.

I mean I know what all the books and psychologists and therapists say, they say there isn't anything wrong with doing that. I'd found it real reassuring to read that it's perfectly normal for a young man to rough up the suspect every once and a while. The only thing I wonder about is what crosses over from being "every once in a while" into "way too much."

I calmed myself by thinking that Chester X was probably sound asleep those very, very, very few times that *that* had happened. And besides, as old as he was, he probably couldn't hear anything anyway, and with my bed on the other side of the room he couldn't be seeing too much, right? I told myself these things, but I only halfway believed them.

He took over the conversation as soon as we were in the room. He pointed at my bed and said, "Sit there, son."

He sat on his bed and asked me, "OK, what are you going to do?"

I looked at him. Before I had a chance to answer he said, "Appears to me that you've got two choices; one, you take my pills from me, tell your mother about this and she'll force me to take injections. Or, two, you throw those pills out and we both escape from here and head on down to Port Saint Lucie before she ends up killing me"—he dropped his voice—"and killing you, too."

He was throwing too much at me at once. Somewhere in my mind I knew I had a whole lot more choices than the two he'd brought up, but I started concentrating on him saying that the Sarge had plans on bumping me off too. I wondered if during all his fake dopiness he'd heard the Sarge say something. You had to see the old bird had some credibility, he'd sure figured out what her plans for him were.

I said, "What do you mean, killing me, too?"

"That got your attention, didn't it? I've seen what's going on here, how you're her handyman and housekeeper and chauffeur and nurse and whipping boy all rolled into one tall, skinny, unhappy, unpaid lump. I've seen how much you hate it, too."

"So what? What's any of that got to do with her trying to kill me? Seems like as much as I do around here I'd be the last one she'd want dead."

Chester X took one of his twisted-up fingers and banged it against his temple three times.

"Wisdom. That's where wisdom comes in. Wisdom is knowledge plus experience, and I've seen how smart you are, Luther, but other than running this joint, you definitely lack any kind of experience. And that makes you a tad light in the wisdom department.

"This isn't anywhere or anyway to be raising a bright

young boy, and even though you do a good job hiding it I can see that's what you are. That's why I'm hoping that you're smart enough and wise enough to listen to someone who can point out what's going to happen to you unless you get on up out of here."

"And what's that? Nothing's gonna happen to me." I couldn't help it, I had to ask, "Why? Did you hear Darnell Dixon say something?"

"I didn't hear that cretin say anything, but what's going to happen is that one day you're going to take over all this, you're going to be the one running all these houses and schemes your mother's got going."

"So? Do you know how much she's worth? You say it like there's something wrong with that. One day I'm gonna have a genuine Jacob Lawrence painting hanging on my walls."

He said, "Don't play stupid with me, young man, I've heard you talking on the phone. I've heard the way you moan and groan to Spunky about—"

"It's Sparky."

"All right, I've heard you crying the blues to Sparky about what she's doing to you. You can see she's got your whole future laid out for you like a map, no mystery, no wondering, no nothing. All of this *is* going to be yours one day, and you'll hate it even more then than you do now."

This was the kind of talk that had gotten Sparky knocked out in front of Taco Bell.

"Your mother is one determined young sister, son, no doubt about it, she's going to get anything and everything she wants. Far as I can tell two of the things she wants the most are you running this operation she's got going and me pushing up daisies somewhere at the same time I'm providing her her financing for her retirement. I'm here to tell you that the only way those two things aren't going to happen is if we aren't around.

"Now I'm going to be honest with you, and I want you to listen carefully and try to understand what I'm saying. I was saving those pills because I'd rather go out all at once than have your mother ease me into a coma and leave me vegetating around here for God knows how long. If anybody's going to have a say as to when my clock gets punched out I'd rather make that call myself than have some lost-soul vampire like your momma doing it for me."

Lost-soul vampire? That had to be the best description of the Sarge I'd ever heard. I smiled. Chester X Stockard was cool, but he still hadn't answered my question.

"You still didn't say how she's going to kill me."

Chester X gave me a disappointed look, sort of like that didn't even need to be asked. "Well," he finally said, "there's different degrees and there's different ways of dying."

I could see where he was going with this: my death was going to be caused by a million small blows spread out over many unhappy years, bla, bla, bla.

I felt relieved. I know it's pretty stupid and paranoid to waste time worrying if your own mother might have plans to kill you, but you never know with the Sarge. She *did* used to say all the time, "I'm the one who brought you into this world and I'd be more than willing to hasten your journey back out." True, she hadn't said it in a couple of years, but knowing the Sarge that could've just been a way to get me to let my guard down, probably so's I wouldn't have any idea when the end was right around the corner.

"Yeah," I told Chester X, "all that's fine, but I'm not going to let you kill yourself with a med overdose while I'm supposed to be watching you."

"Then that means we're going to Port Saint Lucie?"

"To where?"

"It's a beautiful little town on the east coast of Florida, it's where I'm from. It's where my wife and daughters are."

"You've got kin in Florida? The chart says you don't have anybody."

"It's where all my people are buried."

"Oh." I never know how to react when someone says something like that. You feel like you have to say something. I guess I could say "I'm sorry" but that always sounds so insincere, even though I am sorry for their sorrow, if that makes any sense.

So instead I said, "And another thing, how come you're planning on committing suicide? I've seen the charts on you and your finances. If you're so unhappy here I'll help you go to the bank and take some of your cash and get you a ticket down to Florida and you can set yourself up. We can get you out of here so smooth she won't have a clue as to where you went. Man, with three quarters of a million dollars and all those stocks you could get a bad little crib and hire yourself a bad little private nurse. Unless . . . aww, she did it, didn't she? She already got the cash signed over to her."

Chester X laughed. "Looks like I outfoxed myself on this one, doesn't it?"

"She did. She's already got your cash."

"No, son, there never was any money."

"What? I've seen it, she's got your stock certificates and insurance policies and bank accounts."

"Nothing but paper. That's one of the things I love about the Internet, you can buy just about anything. Apparently your mother never bothered to check my stock, if she would've she'd've seen they were all from companies that had gone defunct decades ago. I bought them just before I was about to be sent to the nursing home I was in before this one, place run by white folks."

"What? You really lost me, Mr. X."

"I wanted the white people to believe I had money. They treat you a whole lot better if they think you're well off. I don't know how I ended up in your mother's hands, all I know is I woke up one day and you were standing over me with a razor. And it didn't take long for me to figure out it's no good for me if she thinks I'm loaded. I know she already pulled some sort of hanky-panky to get her hands on some of my government checks."

"So you really don't have a ton of cash?"

"Weight-wise, probably closer to an ounce."

"No seven hundred and fifty thousand dollars?"

"Maybe seven thousand in cash and five or six thousand in stocks."

"Well then, how're your bills getting paid here? This place ain't cheap."

"Social security, my pension and an old-age policy I bought back in the forties."

"Oh, man! The Sarge is going to die! This is great!" I just about slipped and said, "I can't wait for you to kick the bucket so I can see the expression on her face when she finds out you're broke!" But he might have misinterpreted that remark so I caught myself in time.

I said, "Since we're airing out the closet, Mr. X, was it the Black Panthers or the Black Muslims you used to be in?"

He thought for a second, then said, "You know as you age you tend to forget things, but I'm willing to bet I'd've remembered that."

"Then what about your name? How come the chart says you're known as Chester X?"

"You put a lot of faith in those charts, don't you, son?"

"Hey. As far as I'm concerned what's on those charts is more real than reality." It's happening again, I'm using Sarge-Speak and I didn't even mean to.

Chester X said, "The only thing I can figure is that it must have something to do with me having no middle name. I guess writing 'X' was easier than writing 'N.M.N.' "

"So you weren't ever a militant, you didn't fight in the black liberation movement?"

He laughed. "I think being a militant is sort of like being a philosopher—they both sound good, but the pay is lousy. I worked on the railroad."

I let his comment slide. What did he know? I can't see America not taking good care of its best-known and best-loved philosopher. "The railroad, huh?"

149

"That's right, put all those decades in, then they forced me out. I'm getting the last laugh, though, they cut me loose and gave me a gold-plated watch, sort of so's I could count the hours until I died, but I outlasted it, cheap thing gave out four years ago." Chester X thought this was very funny.

"So you never met Rap or Stokely or Angela or Huey?" Mr. Kamari's black history class was paying off.

He thought for a second. " 'Fraid not. Had a cousin once by the name of Huey, and wooed a gal called herself Angela, though. Sorry to disappoint you."

"And here I've been giving you extra-good care 'cause I thought you were one of the O.G.'s of the revolution."

"I'm a member of the Brotherhood of Sleeping Car Porters, it wouldn't be too much of a stretch to say we were revolutionaries in our time. Seems to me that that should be enough for me to keep on getting this extra-good care you've been doling out." He brought one of his twisted-up hands to his jaw and rubbed. "I've got to admit, you do give one great shave!

"Look," he said, "I've done a lot of thinking on this, we can—"

I knew where this was headed. I butted in. "Mr. Stockard, I'm not going to any Florida, and neither are you. I'll tell you what I will do, though, I'll keep these pills and that mattress you vandalized to myself, the Sarge won't know anything about them. But you're still going to have to keep the zombie act up when she's around, otherwise she *will* put you on the needle."

Chester X started looking desperate, and it was a very

funny feeling for me. It's really hard to see someone you thought was out of it having so many emotions.

"But, son," he said, "your life would be so much happier in Florida, happier and healthier. Why, all that fruit and sunshine can work wonders on someone's skin."

No he didn't!

He kept going. "Think about it, I've seen how you work like a dog on that science fair project, I've seen how much you study, I've seen your grades, you'd be able to finish school, then get into a good college and do the things you want to do. That's not going to happen here. She can't afford to let you go off to college for four years, who'd run these places for her? Do you realize how much she'd have to pay someone to do everything that you do?"

"Don't worry, I'm getting paid. It's all going into my education fund. I might not have any cash flow now, but I keep track of my hours and she deposits my money for me. I'll have way over a hundred thousand for school by the time I'm eighteen. And so what? If push comes to shove I can stay here and go to the U of M—Flint."

He said, "But, Luther—"

I told him, "Mr. Stockard, you'd best forget about us going to Florida, it ain't in the stars."

"Aww, Luther," he said, "you really ought to think about it, and besides, have you ever met any Florida women?"

Oh. I knew what was next, I'm supposed to be such a loser with the women up here that I'd have better luck in Florida.

"They're different down home," he said. "Warm-weather

women are a lot friendlier, a lot easier to get along with. You'd meet some fine young woman in no time at all. Seems from my experience Southern women are a lot more loving. A lot more comforting, if you get my gist."

I got his gist, whatever that is, and all it did was make me wonder what the people of Florida would say if they knew their state was being promoted as Ho-ville, U.S.A.?

I said, "That's cool, Mr. X, but you'd best forget me and you going to Florida, the closest I'm getting to anything Floridian is in the fruit bowl upstairs."

Chester X didn't appreciate the beautiful irony of that remark. His eyes got hard and drilled into my head. Then he let me have it with both barrels.

He said, "I can't understand it, especially from a young man like you, someone who obviously likes to take matters into his own hands, so to speak. Don't be such a jerk, Luther."

Aw, no. This can't be happening!

This is what I call one of those "branded" moments. They got these shows on the Western Network where the cowboys run a steer down and tie its feet together before they take a red-hot branding iron and poke it into the cow's behind. You can bet that if that cow lives to be a thousand years old he'll still have that mark, both on his hide and on his soul.

Chester X might as well have snatched a glowing orange poker right out of the campfire and mashed that baby right onto my brain, because I knew I'd be carrying the embarrassment and humiliation of the words "jerk" and "like to take matters in your own hands" around with me for the rest of my life. And if reincarnation is real I'll probably be taking them into my next seven or eight lives, too.

I'm pretty sure I was maintaining my usual cool on the outside, but just like when those cowboys brand that steer and it doesn't seem to give much more than a sad "Mooo," on the inside my heart and mind were filled with smoke and wild, rolling eyes and the nasty smell of singed, melting hair.

Chester X was out for blood! If he'd stoop this low who knows where he'd stop? What if he had pictures!

Thank God I didn't have to find out—the phone rang upstairs. I said, "Uh, I've got to get that. We'll talk about this a little later." I tore away from my room to answer the phone.

I hope Chester X didn't take me too seriously about carrying this heart-to-heart talk on later. If he held his breath waiting for that to happen he wouldn't have to worry about saving up any pills!

· 12 ·

RIGHTFULLY GOLD!

It's a good thing I have a very high threshold for humiliation. Besides, I had more important things to do than worry about what Chester X thought he might have seen. If I didn't come up with a whole load of fresh angles on this science fair project the dream for the three-peat would die.

My research and presentation were all tight. I had my hypothesis that I needed to test and I'd set up the experimentation process of the project. I had the kind of title that reached out and grabbed your attention: "Are Our Children Being Poisoned Right Under Our Noses?" And I'd talked to Lucas Sorge, the class computer geek, and was sneaking money out of petty cash to pay him to set up a bad PowerPoint presentation. Everything was tight but I felt like I needed one or two things more to put it over the top, one or two things that would knock Shayla Patrick's little know-it-all behind right out of the box.

In my current fragile state of mind I can't go through the drama of last year's science fair again, and even though I won it, that's one experience that taught me that I don't handle failing, or coming close to failing, real good.

Just a year ago I was sure I was going to win for the second year in a row. Until the day of the previews of everybody's project.

I'd walked through the gym and checked everything out. Most of them were so lame that they'd lose to a baking-soda-and-vinegar volcano.

Even though they were lame I'd tell whoever made them, "That's tight, good luck at the judging tomorrow, I'm sure you've got a good chance at winning." It's all right to offer hope to people who didn't have a chance; they should get something for their efforts.

Then I saw Shayla's project and the truth hit me; mine was good, but hers was better. Not just a little better, but way, way, way better.

And the worst thing was that she knew it and knew that I knew it too.

Shayla and Eloise Exum walked by my project and Shayla read my displays and looked through my slides and had the nerve to let out a sigh of relief. She looked at me through those thick, black, beautiful eyelashes and said, "That's really good, Luther."

If you look at just the words you might not understand their real meaning, you might not see what was really happening. You had to listen real hard, and even kind of imagine it, but if you really wanted to hear it, it was there, that taunting tone that she only halfway tried to keep out of her voice. And then there was the way she smiled when she said it. If you really look at a smile it ain't nothing but a showing of teeth, and I've watched the Nature Channel enough to know that tooth showing is nothing but an act of aggression.

Then she really did it, her smile got even more aggressive and she said, "Good luck at the judging tomorrow, I'm sure you've got a good chance of winning."

Aw, no. No she didn't!

She's even throwing at me the same line I use on the losers! In my book there's nothing worse than being hypocritical or two-faced and when you add that to all of Shayla's other character flaws she was just too much to take.

All I could think to do was put my nose in the air, sniff real loud and say, "What's that I smell?" Sniff, sniff. "Did someone open a can of embalming fluid in here?" A tight comeback, but probably not the kind of thing you want to say to the woman of your dreams.

I was completely depressed. All I wanted to do was figure out a way to break into the school that night and destroy her project. I might've done it too, but with her project being called "A Demonstration on the Problems of Nuclear Waste" I was afraid I might mess around and get myself radiated. And if I did that what would Miss Madagascar say?

I stopped by the Sarge's house on my way home for my daily briefing. I thought I was being on the down-low but she picked up on something right away.

"What's eating you?"

Maybe it's a mother-child thing, maybe when me and Miss Madagascar get together and start populating the earth with sturdy little African children I'll know more about it but for now I can't understand how the Sarge knows whenever something is bothering me. I can try to be as cool with it as possible but it seems like when I come near her I'm wearing a big sign that says Troubled.

I told her, "Nothing."

"Look, I don't have time for games, either tell me or don't, but don't fall off into that I-gotta-pull-teeth-to-get-the-information thing."

"It's really nothing, I just don't think I'm going to win the science fair this year."

Her eyes rolled.

"You don't have to tell me, I know, that's sucker path action."

She said, "You said it, not me. But what makes you so sure you're not going to win?"

I said, "Shayla Patrick. I don't know how, but I swear her father must've hired some professional help with her project, there's no way a kid coulda put that thing together alone."

"So you get some professional help next year and beat her back."

"I want to win first place a second time in a row. I've already got a spot set up to hang this year's first-place medal on my wall and then I can win next year's and have a three-peat going."

When you say things like this you have to be careful not to sound whiny, I mean between the new hormones and me faking it some of the time I was getting a lot of bass in my voice and I usually remember to keep it nice and low, but say something like this and your voice can't help cracking, then getting weak.

She sighed and looked at me. "Is Bea Scott still the head of science and math at your school?"

"Yes." Ms. Scott was close to four thousand years old and they were forcing her out because her mind was like the transmission of a 1973 Buick, sometimes it would go into drive but most times it was good and comfortable just sitting in park.

"So she's still the one who judges the science fairs?"

"Yes, but this is the last year she's doing it, they're making her quit."

The Sarge told me, "Go get your crew ready for swimming. Quit worrying about nonsense like that stupid project, that's not what's important in life."

I knew more was going to come. That's not the way the Sarge ends a conversation.

She said, "You know what? I'ma use this as a lesson to show you what kind of things really are worth you expending your energies on."

Uh-oh! "What does that mean?"

"Look," she said, "I know you and I don't see eye to eye on a lot of things, and I'm not going to ascribe it all to the fact that you're extremely immature for your age or that you still look at things with a naivete that long ago lost its charm.

"I know that people can have different philosophies about life. That's one of the things that makes it interesting. We can honestly disagree about things and that doesn't mean I'm necessarily right each and every time and you're always wrong. Ninety-nine times out of a hundred, yes, but there always is that other time."

The sad thing about this is that she was dead serious.

"I know you're into philosophy so let me share a little something with you, something that if you choose to pay attention to will do a lot to make your life a whole lot smoother. But of course I know it's one of those things that's going to go smack into your right ear hole, then come barreling out of your left. But at least you won't have the excuse of saying you've never been told."

I felt like getting a Q-tip to clean my ears so this great information she was about to share would have a smooth and easy path to barrel out of the left side of my head.

"Now, you may not believe it, you may want to make things more complex than they are, but believe me, the truth is out there, and it's very simple.

"Since you're one who likes to throw all those trite pseudophilosophical sayings into your conversation, let me throw one right back at you. Do you know what saying I'm talking about?"

I thought, very quietly and very carefully, "Could it be 'There's no fool like an old fool'?"

But I said, "No, I don't."

She said, "The saying is 'It's not what you know that's important, it's who you know.'"

The soulfully deep stare let me know I was supposed to be impressed.

Nice try.

"You hold on for a little while and if you're anywhere near as bright as you think you are you'll see the importance of that saying. Need I say more?"

I said, "No," and let the subject drop because lots of times her lessons never come true and even when they do they're not anything that I'd want to learn.

I didn't think about the Sarge's lesson again until the prize day for last year's science fair. I woke up dreading having to turn my title over to Shayla Patrick, but I had to go and face the music like the man that I am. I just hoped I wouldn't cry when I got called up onstage to get second prize.

Me and Shayla were in third hour together and you'da thought she was getting ready to win the Interstate Lotto Jackpot instead of stupid first prize in a stupid middle school science fair in a stupid little city. She had her locks down and they and she were about the most beautiful and repulsive things I'd ever seen.

She and Eloise Exum giggled and whispered all through class and I couldn't understand why Ms. Warren let them get away with it. I mean any fool could see that their behavior was disrupting the class.

With the award ceremony being next period it seemed like if it didn't hurry up and come Shayla was going to explode.

When we got to the auditorium three people's projects were on the stage. Bo Travis's, my weak mess, and, fresh from the crypt, Shayla's. Even though if she was going to be fair about it she would've had to give most of the credit to whatever rocket scientist and Nobel Peace Prize for

160

Science winner her no-good rich daddy had paid to put it together for her.

Ms. Scott came out looking even more shaky and confused than she usually does and said all the right words, the teachers were so proud, we have such great futures, life is wonderful and on and on with the words that were just designed to stop us losers from facing up to the fact that we were losers.

Then she said, "Would the following three students please come onto the stage? Bo Travis." Somebody yelled out, "Nice uniform, Bo, where's your hat?"

Ms. Scott said, "Shayla Patrick." About nine girls clapped and whistled and cheered.

"And Luther T. Farrell." Someone made a loud fart sound.

As I slinked onto the stage I thought to all those losers in the auditorium, "Go ahead, don't recognize, hate, but you're not going to be disappointed, you're gonna see the greatest humiliation in the life and times of Luther T. Farrell."

I put my head down as Ms. Scott shook Bo's hand, then Shayla's. It wasn't until later that I remembered she never even offered her hand to me.

The three of us faced the spotlights. Bo was standing as quiet as ever. Shayla was out of control with joy but she was doing a great job to keep it under wraps.

Between classes she'd changed into a long African dress and had her locks pinned up with this bad purple and black scarf holding them in place.

And her smile. With the stage lights on her and her

teeth so white and shiny, and her lips so full and dark and kissable-looking with just the hint of a lightly shiny lipstick on them, and with her long fingers gracefully twined together in front of her, and something sparkly all over her eyelids and cheeks, I knew I was doomed to be in love with someone who I couldn't talk to without insulting her. I finally understood what that great philosopher, whose name escapes me at the moment, meant when she said, "Love stinks."

Old Lady Scott said, "In third place is a fine job done by Mr. Bo Travis."

When she handed him his medal Bo nodded at her once and put it around his neck. No smile, no wave, no nothing.

Shayla grinned and clapped as loud as she could and gave him a big hug.

Well, maybe something good was gonna come out of this after all. At least I'd finally not have to imagine what it felt like to be wrapped up in the loving arms of Ms. Shayla Night of the Living Dead Patrick.

Ms. Scott cleared her throat. "And to the second-place winner, please don't be discouraged, remember that the world can be unfair, but also keep in mind that the world needs young people like you who can create something as beautiful as this."

She was going a little overboard. My project was good, but even I wouldn't've called it beautiful.

Then she said, "And for second place, Ms. Shayla Patrick."

The audience gasped. Eloise Exum stood up in the front row and yelled, "No you didn't! You know that's not right!"

Ms. Scott and Shayla hugged and cried. Ms. Scott was whispering something to Shayla.

I'd won.

I'd won!

Don't ask me how, but I'd won for the second year in a row!

For a second I thought about the Sarge, about how she said who you know is more important than what you know. I wish she could've been here to see how wrong she was. But just as quick I forgot all about her and my heart was squeezed with joy!

I threw my hands up in the air and yelled, "Yes! Yes! How you like me now?"

Ms. Scott and Shayla finally let go of each other. Ms. Scott said, "Luther Farrell, I'd like to prevent you . . ." She paused. "I'd like to *present* you with this year's first place in the science fair."

It was like I went into a trance. Shayla shook my hand, then sat down and smiled bravely as I walked up to the podium. Ms. Scott reached the gold medal out to me and before I had a chance to take it, it fell to the stage floor.

I bent down to pick it up and reached it toward the lights. There'd be another nail going into my bedroom wall tonight!

I couldn't remember the rest of the day at school. The medal burned in my pocket like a wad of benjamins.

When I finally got to the home I showed my medal to my crew.

"Is it real gold?" Mr. Baker asked. "Looks fake to me."

I answered, "It might as well be real gold, it's worth as much."

"Good work, Luther," Mr. Foster said. "And in celebration I guess this means you can spring for some Häagen Dazs Caramel Cone Explosion ice cream for dessert tonight instead of that ice-milk crap your mother's been foisting on us lately."

I laughed. "I guess so, let me go put this medal on the wall and then we'll head out to the store."

I ran down to the basement and stopped in the utility room to get the hammer and one of the shiny brass nails. A gold medal deserves at least a gold-looking nail.

As I stood holding the hammer and nail and gold medal I paused to do some musing. You know, there's something especially lonely about a gold medal hanging all by itself on a bedroom wall, something that says "fluke," or "beginner's luck," or "one in a million," but two gold medals, now that says something completely different. That says, "Oh, yeah, baby, this is the real deal!"

I put the nail in my mouth, stepped up on my bed and did a double take. Right next to my first medal there already was another nail. This mystery nail was just a regular old nail, it wasn't gold.

This must be some kind of a sign. Maybe someone was trying to tell me that there was now the possibility that I could win the science fair three times in a row.

I put the new medal on the old nail and hammered the new nail next to them both.

"Be patient," I told the gold nail, "in three hundred and sixty-four days you'll have gold hanging from you, too!"

13

WHO'S YOUR DADDY?

Me and Darnell and the Sarge had just finished one of our old family traditions: we'd gone to the Food Club and done the month's shopping for the homes. Darnell parked the Happy Neighbor Group Home van at the front door and I got out and began unloading groceries. The Sarge got out of the van, looked through the window into the dayroom and was just *this* far from actually laughing.

She said to Darnell, "Have you ever seen those magazines where they show you a picture and you have to supply a funny caption explaining what it's all about?"

I knew whatever this was about it wasn't going to be funny to me. I'd read somewhere that there's always a whiff of tragedy in humor, and the couple of times I'd heard the Sarge try to crack a joke the humor didn't have whiffs of tragedy, it *stank* of tragedy. Darnell said, "Yeah."

She said, "For this picture"—she pointed through the window into the dayroom—"I'd have these two television executives looking through a two-way mirror and one says to the other, 'From our initial test audiences it looks like this new program might have some serious quality problems!'"

Darnell looked in the window and broke out laughing. It seemed like a real laugh too, not the usual behind-kissing one he had for everything the Sarge said.

She said to me, "Unless I'm mistaken, I think you're needed."

I didn't even bother looking, I just lugged the crates of macaroni and cheese and ramen noodles into the kitchen. As soon as I set the first one down Mr. Foster came up to me and said, "Sorry to be the bearer of bad news, Luther, but he did it again."

Aw, no! This can't be happening!

When I got near the dayroom my nose told me what he was talking about.

Mr. Baker had fired another shot in this war me and him had been having. We'd been beefing 'cause about a year ago Mr. DuBois, the Sarge's quack lawyer, had convinced her to follow state law and make everybody in her homes stop smoking. Most of the clients were OK with it after a while, but Mr. Baker let everyone know he'd been smoking since he was in his momma's womb so he wasn't about to stop for some stupid state law. Plus, there was the little thing of the people at the rehab center and Darnell Dixon and the Sarge giving him cigarettes every once in a while, just enough to keep his tobacco jones alive.

His way of getting revenge for not being able to smoke

24/7 was to mess his pants up 'cause he knew I was going to be the one who had to clean him. Since it was me who had to enforce the new no smoking rule, he figured who better to hit back at?

I'm not going to lie, at first I did feel a little sympathetic for what he was going through, I mean the poor man had been a nicotine addict most of his life and then the Sarge cut out ninety-nine percent of his smokes. That didn't seem fair, but it didn't seem fair that he'd try to get at me for what she'd done to him, so my sympathy had worn out a long time ago.

I'd even sneaked some money out of the petty cash and paid Dr. Mark to write him a script for some Stop-Smoke gum, but right after I got the script filled I came home from school and Mr. Baker was bouncing off the walls. He had a coconut-sized wad in his mouth and had chewed all twenty pieces of the gum at one time.

When nothing seemed to work and he kept dropping these loads in his pants for me, I'd told the Sarge she should toss Mr. Baker out and find him another placement, but she threw another Sargeism at me.

"Don't you think you're being a little harsh?" she'd asked. "Or have you even bothered to think what his life would be like if he had to leave here? The time that he's been under your wing is the first time in thirty-five years of institutional care that he hasn't had to be in restraints most of the day. Give him a break, the man likes you, go look at his records, he's done a lot worse."

The real reason she wouldn't get rid of him was that she

could use him as what DuBois called plausible deniability for the suspicious fires that happened to pop up in any of the rental houses that she wanted to get rid of.

Strange as it might seem, if she had Mr. Baker transferred to one of her rental houses you didn't have to be watching the Psychic Lifeline Channel to know that within a few weeks that baby would be going up like gasoline-soaked rags at a pyromaniacs' convention.

I followed Mr. Foster into the dayroom and knew I was right in not wasting my time looking to see what the Sarge had made that weak joke about.

Mr. Baker had stunk the room up so bad that all of the Crew was sitting there with their eyes glued to the TV and their thumbs and pointing fingers squeezing their noses shut.

Ha, ha, ha, big joke. "Looks like this show might have some serious quality problems."

As soon as he saw me, Mr. Baker threw one hand up in the air like he was halting traffic and started repeating, "What can I say, I gotta smoke." Even he was pinching his nose closed.

What's the point in getting mad? Nobody else was going to clean him up, and the sooner I got him wiped down and showered the sooner this funk would leave the dayroom and I could get some hours in on my science fair project, finish my homework and get me and the Crew to bed.

I pretended this wasn't nothing and started breathing out of my mouth so the smell wouldn't gag me.

"OK, Mr. Baykah, into da shower. Ged 'em off and leab 'em by da doe."

Mr. Foster said, "We want to give you our deepest and most abiding thanks for taking care of this matter, Luther."

Mr. Baker said, "I think a cigarette would really help me now."

"Not today it won't."

"It would, I gotta smoke now!"

I steered him to the bathroom.

He knew the drill. He took all his clothes off and dropped them outside the bathroom door, then turned on the shower and adjusted it to his regular temperature, about two degrees above ice cold. As punishment at the home he'd been in before he came to me, whenever he did anything wrong they used to hose him down with freezing water. Over the years I guess he'd come to think that was what a shower was all about so he only took icy cold ones.

He stood there shivering and goose-pimpling up with the water running over him. I set the commode seat in the shower and had him sit on it. I used the handheld hose to clean him off, had him scrub himself, then pulled on a pair of rubber gloves and picked up his pants and underpants.

Mr. Baker said, "Call that idiot Darnell Dixon and tell him I want that cigarette he promised me."

"I'm not calling Darnell and you aren't smoking anything."

"Oh yeah," he said, "you watch me, before this night's through *something's* gonna be smoking in this house."

I rinsed his pants and drawers out.

I got Mr. Baker all cleaned up, put his clothes right in the washer, took my own shower, cleaned the stall, got the Crew's MREs ready, fed them, cleaned up the table, put the dishes in the dishwasher, gave them their dessert, gave them their meds, put Mr. Baker's clothes in the dryer, sprayed air freshener in the dayroom, turned on the TV, got them all settled, let them watch half an hour of TV, got them all to bed, finished my homework and my science fair project for the night, then went down to my room.

I was being real careful around Chester X since we'd had our heart-to-heart talk. Not only because I knew he'd been awake when he should've been asleep, but also because I was feeling a little bad about how I'd treated him back when I thought he was out of it. It had me thinking about how I treated all of the Crew.

Don't get me wrong, I've been to a lot of different group homes and seen how bad the clients get treated, I've never done anything really bad to my crew, I mean I always talk to all of them like maybe there's a chance they're understanding what's being said. But that was the problem, instead of acting like *maybe* there was a chance I should've been acting like they really did understand. It might not seem like much of a change, but it was.

So I was being real careful how I talked to everybody now, especially Chester X.

When I got into my room he was in bed with the covers tucked under his chin pretending he was null and void, just in case the Sarge was making an inspection.

I said, "All clear, Mr. X."

He said, "Mr. Baker left you another surprise, that's why I had to give up on TV."

I told him, "I know, I got it all taken care of."

170

He pulled the covers down and climbed out of bed. He already had the card table set up.

This was another change since we'd had our heart-to-heart. It seemed like he thought since I knew he was aware of what was going on I had to entertain Chester X and talk to him a lot more. So me and him had been playing cards until eleven or twelve every night. Most of the time we played tunk.

When I'd come into the basement at the end of the day he'd have the chairs and table waiting for me. In the middle of the table there'd be a deck of cards and next to where I sat he'd have my jelly jar full of quarters with the top already off. He told me that way I wouldn't have to expend any energy constantly taking the top off every time I lost.

On his side of the table he always started with one quarter. He said it was in case I had beginner's luck.

He eased himself into his spot and started shuffling the cards. For being old as he is he has real good hands when it comes to shuffling.

"So what's the word today, Luther?"

"You don't know, and you don't want to know, Mr. X."

I cut the cards.

He said, "Couldn'ta been that bad."

"Says who?"

He dealt and said, "Luther, if it wasn't for two certain women you wouldn't have any problems, would you? Which one of them was it today?"

"Shayla."

He said, "Son, I'm not one to get into your business, but why don't you just try being nice to the girl? Why don't you let her know how you feel? She might surprise you."

"Yeah. Right."

He spread his cards and said, "Fourteen."

I had thirty-six. I dug two quarters out of the jar and he slid them over into his pile.

I think he lets me win one or two out of every ten or fifteen hands just so I won't get too discouraged and quit.

Chester X said, "I'm serious, sounds to me like you two are trying to get a spark going but neither one of you knows how. And I'm not trying to be funny, Luther, but I think a lot of the problem is you."

I had to be careful. Although me and Chester X had got kind of cool I still think some of the time he was playing mind games with me and trying to distract me from my cards.

I said, "Wha-a-a-t?" And shuffled the cards. They just wouldn't dance in my hands the way they did in his.

He said, "No, seriously. I just don't think you've got enough self-confidence. And, Luther, I'm telling you, that's what folks find irresistible about other folks, confidence. And don't confuse that with cockiness, either, I'm talking about a healthy dose of self-respect and confidence.

"Take me, for example, even though I've spent many years being considered pretty dapper and witty, I've never thought that those were the main things that kept me with a whole bevy of female company."

I dealt each of us five cards and pretended I was surprised. "I can't see how they could see anything beyond your wit and your dapperness, Mr. X."

He said, "Scoff if you want, but I think it's the confidence." He winked. "Don't take it personal, but even some of the plug-ugly fellas I knew did OK with the women if they had confidence."

Chester X sure does like to dis folks in his conversation, but he always smiles when he fires these shots.

I said, "Thanks for the advice, Mr. X, but I don't really have a problem when it comes to the honeys. It ain't that kind of party. What I have here is a failure to communicate." That was a line from a movie I'd just seen on the Classic Movie Channel.

He said, "Go on, this is a good first step. Knowing you've got a problem, or as you like to call it, a failure, is the first step to solving it." He spread the four, five, and six of hearts.

I shook my head and said, "I saw this documentary on the Wacky World of Nature Network about animal mating rituals. It was called something like 'Animals Are Just Like Me and You, They Like to Get Their Freak On Too' and it was all about courtship and getting a mate, mostly with birds. It was about how the male birds have to put on what they call a courting display before the females will give them any kind of play.

"When the male birds broke into this display thing it looked like they were throwing a fit or something. They were jerking and flapping and twitching and carrying on in a way that wouldn't make anyone or anything think about sex. It looked like they were completely out of control, it looked like someone had just nicked them with a pellet gun."

I drew a card and threw out the eight of clubs. I told him, "But not to the female birds, uh-uh, they thought this bumping around was hot! But, and here's where it ties in to me, Mr. X, it only looked like twitching to those who didn't understand that the dancing was giving the females all kinds of signals about the male's health and strength and how tough he was between the sheets. It was all about letting the female birds know if the male was good enough to be her baby's daddy."

Chester X went down. I slid him another quarter and the deck.

"And," I said, "if there was one thing wrong with the way the male bird danced, if he stuck his right wing out instead of his left, or if he scratched the dirt with three toes instead of two, or if he looked north for just a second too long, that was it. The females went deep into hate-eration on him. One little step in the wrong direction or one feather out of place and she'd be through with him. He'd be dancing solo that night."

Chester X cleared his throat and said, "Not that there's anything wrong with dancing solo every once in a while."

I wonder how long I'ma have to listen to comments like that.

Chester X shuffled the cards so smooth it looked like they'd turned liquid and he was pouring them from one hand to the other.

"Anyway. That's my little difficulty, Mr. X, for some

reason I can't seem to get the real 4-1-1 about Luther T. Farrell across to Shayla. It's like I'm kicking my toes up at the wrong time or bobbing my head to the right when I should be bobbing it to the left. I don't know exactly what it is but it's just one little thing, one stupid thing that has her reading me as lame."

Chester X dealt the cards again. I picked up my hand, it totaled twenty; most times a good low go-down number. I said, "Twenty!" And spread my cards.

He said, "You got me," and slid two quarters across the table to me.

I picked up the deck and he slid his cards over to me without showing them.

I said, "What'd you have?"

He said, "Uh, I'm not sure." He tried to put the cards back in the deck but I checked them anyway. He had nineteen! He'd won and was letting me take the pot!

I said, "Aw, Mr. X, that's so disrespectful, how you just gonna let me win like that? What's the point in playing? I mean I know every night after you beat me you put my quarters back in the jar the next morning, but come on, at least you could front that I got a chance."

"Luther, I wasn't intending to be disrespectful, it's just that you were looking so down that I thought losing fourteen or fifteen hands in a row would've been a little too hard on you right now, son.

"But doesn't what you're talking about with birds boil down to a lack of confidence? Aren't you approaching that young lady with the thought that you aren't going to do something right, that no matter what you say or do she's going to look at it as you having your wings up instead of down?"

I said, "It's more complicated nowadays. It's not like when you were young."

Chester X said, "I understand more than you think I do, Luther, and I understand things are pretty much exactly like they were when I was your age. Don't you think I said those exact words you just said to me to my father? And don't you think my father said the same thing to his father? And don't you think my father's father said the same things to his father?"

I was afraid he was going to run this all the way back to Fred Flintstone and Barney Rubble.

"And I understand that it feels to you like you're the first young man who's ever had his nose opened up by a woman before, but, son, believe—"

I've learned I have to stop Mr. X when he starts busting out these sayings from the eighteenth century. I'd let "bevy" get by, but this sounded too interesting. I said, "What's that mean? What's having your nose opened up by a woman mean?"

"It means you're so far under her spell that she can easily lead you around by the nose if she wants to."

"Oh."

He wasn't through. He had to go and paint a clearer picture of the saying. "With the way Shayla's got you moping and carrying on and groaning, we'd say, back in the day, that she's got your nose so far open, Luther, that you could smell Fidel barbecuing steaks down in Havana."

"Ha ha."

"Quit interrupting me, you're throwing me off my line of thought. As I was saying, you're not the first young man to be crushed by some sweet young girl, it happens all the time, Luther. But if you would just take stock in yourself and see what it is you've got going for you maybe someone else would see it too."

I shuffled the cards and started dealing.

I said, "I know I've got a lot going for me, I don't know anyone else in Flint who's my age who've got their own ride and their own credit cards and their own—"

Chester X slammed his hand down on the table. The pile of quarters he'd taken from me jumped up and wobbled before they settled back down. He said, "No! That's not what I'm talking about at all! That's your mother talking, that's not you!"

Ever since I'd told him we weren't going to make a break for Florida he'd been sending little torpedoes at the Sarge to let me know how bad she was for me.

He said, "What I'm talking about here is *you*, not what you have.

"Let me tell you some of the other things I understand about you, young man. I understand the fact that you're respectful, you're kind, you're considerate, you're funny; unintentionally most of the time, but I take my laughs wherever I can get them these days."

He started ticking these things off on his fingers.

"I understand how smart you are, how ambitious you are, and I also understand that while you aren't exactly the easiest thing on the eyes, I have seen worse." He winked and smiled, but I knew out of this whole pep talk those words would be the ones I'd remember the clearest. This was the main part that would be branded into my mind.

He kept going. "And I also understand that the most impressive part of the whole Luther T. Farrell package is that you've accomplished all of this in spite of the fact that you've had very little positive adult influence or guidance. You've managed to turn yourself into a very decent human being even though, as far as I can see, you've used nothing but that TV in the dayroom and your own mind to do it. Your mother has been negligent in many ways."

There it was. Night after night the conversation always got twisted around to the Sarge and how the best thing for me to do was to run on down to Florida with him. Some of the things he said I'd have to do a little musing about, but what he *didn't* understand was that Luther T. Farrell is a fighter, not a runner.

He said, "I was watching the Sea Life Network yesterday and there was a lesson in it for you, Luther. It was about this sea slug that's got a tiny, tiny brain that the slug uses only one time in its life. It uses it to move from where it was born to another area just a little bit away; then it anchors itself to a rock and it'll never use that brain again. So you know what it does? It eats its own brain. It absorbs its own brain, it uses it for enough energy until it's established in this new place.

"That's you! If you don't get out of here you're going to put down roots and dissolve your brain and turn into the Sarge, Part Two."

I said, "Whoops! How'd I know the Sarge was going to be making a special guest appearance on this CD?"

He laughed. "See what I mean? See how smart you are? Here I've been thinking I was slick and you've known my plan all along."

He slid the pile of quarters that he'd won back over to me and said, "Here, save me the trouble of putting them back in the jar in the morning."

I said, "That I can do, but don't think that's gonna get you any closer to Florida."

He laughed and said, "Don't make me go to plan B on you, Mr. Man."

"And what's that?"

"I was only going to tell you as a last resort, but it looks like since you've figured me out I'm going to have to show my hole card."

I said, "I can't wait to see."

"Well," Mr. X. said, "it would be a good way to demonstrate what we've been talking about so I'm going to go ahead and tell you.

"I've been thinking it over and I've decided I'm going to Florida. With you or without you."

I said, "That sounds fair."

He said, "No, what's fair is that I let you know how I'm going to get there if you don't come."

"I'm listening."

"You think I was joking about the confidence thing, don't you? You think I was pulling your leg when I said that a man or woman with confidence is irresistible, don't you?"

I said, "I can't say I thought you were joking, I was thinking you were straight-up wrong."

Chester X said, "Just to show you how right I am I'm going to bring this demonstration real close to home for you. Maybe a little painfully close."

Uh-oh.

He smiled. "That's right! I've been noticing how your momma comes in and inspects us every night before she drives back to her place. And I've been noticing that she looks at me a little bit differently than she looks at everyone else."

I busted out laughing! "That's 'cause she thinks you're bling-bling, if she knew how broke you are you'd get the same dirty look that Mr. Foster does."

"Spoken like a young man whose confidence tank is on empty! There's lots more to it than that, I know when a woman is giving me the eye, and the way your momma looks at me is starting to reactivate these old bones!"

That was enough for me! I was starting to get all kinds of real disturbing pictures in my mind that would interfere with my sleep. I got up from the table and got in bed.

I said, "Don't make me sick, Mr. X."

Chester X got back in his bed and kept his little head poked out of the covers to keep shooting this nonsense at me.

"Oh," he said, "I see, it's because your mother's such a hot young thing and I'm so old, huh? But what's that old song say? 'Age ain't nothing but a number.'

"So don't say I didn't warn you. One of these days after you've given me a really good shave and I've splashed on some of my Old Spice and borrowed some of those jeans you wear around your knees I just might have to start courting your momma. And after I marry her I'm taking some of her money and heading south.

"I'm giving you a choice. Either come with me to Port Saint Lucie now or the next time one of your partners asks you 'Who's your daddy?' you'd best start practicing saying Chester No Middle Name Stockard. One way or the other I'm getting out of here."

I turned off the light and said, "Well, I can't say I wasn't warned, can I?"

Mr. X said, "Good night, son."

I laughed. "Good night . . . Daddy."

Chester X said, "What is it that your boy Spunky is always telling you? 'Don't hate, congratulate.'"

I didn't even have to look at the clock, I knew it was *way past* my bedtime.

14

THE ORDER OF THE UNIVERSE
MAINTAINED

I can think of a lot better ways to start a day other than coming out of a good sleep and seeing Chester X standing over you. But that was the hand I'd been dealt.

"Luther? Rise and shine, you just about slept through the alarm again."

Aww, no! Not today! Today was the day they announced the science fair results.

I went into the bathroom and looked at my chin. "Mr. X, could you come here a minute?"

Chester X popped his head into the bathroom. "What is it?"

"Should I shave my goatee or let it go?"

Chester X squinted at me. "Your what? I didn't know you had a goatee. Here, let me see."

He tilted my chin back. "Luther, I think you're being

pretty generous to call this a goatee, I can't see more than a hair or two in there."

"I didn't ask you to judge it, Mr. X, I just wanted your advice on whether I should shave it off."

He said, "I think putting a razor on that isn't anything but asking for trouble. Why don't you pluck them out? It'll take you all of two seconds."

"What, pluck it like a girl?"

"No, pluck it like someone who's got sense enough not to shave that hash you got going there. Splash a little of my Old Spice on afterwards and you'll be good to go."

I looked at the goatee again. "You got any tweezers?"

By quarter to eight I took care of my personal business and had all of the Crew up, fed, medicated, cleaned, shaved and waiting to go to the vocational center.

When I dropped them Chester X squeezed my shoulder and said, "OK, son, best of luck with your project. Just remember, if you did the best you could, you did the best you could."

"Thanks, Mr. X, but this baby's sewed up. Remember what you told me, confidence."

He said, "Being confident's good, but let's not go overboard."

"Mr. X," I said, "you get ready to celebrate tonight."

I wish I felt as confident as I was fronting to Mr. X. Inside I was shook. They weren't doing any previews of the projects this year but from what I'd seen and heard Shayla's was just as tough as last year.

By fourth hour it was getting hard to breathe.

Then right in the middle of Ms. Warren's class an announcement came on the PA: "Luther T. Farrell, please report to the main office immediately."

I went down to the office and Mrs. Vickers said, "Go right on in, Luther. How's your mom doing? Tell her I asked after her."

I walked into Old Man Brown's office.

"Mr. Farrell, please have a seat, I'll be with you in a moment."

Sure enough, Brown started right in on the mind games with me. He pointed at the chair that faced his desk. It was one of those little kiddie chairs, nothing but a tiny metal h-shaped frame with two pieces of thin plywood attached to it.

No matter how hard you tried to be, no matter how tough, after two minutes of squirming around on that little chair you felt like the biggest idiot in the world, which was the whole point.

I squatted on the chair and waited.

He hung the phone up and said, "Now, let's see, what do I owe the pleasure of this visit to?"

I shrugged.

He said, "Here's a surprise, this is good news. It's about the science fair."

What?

"I won?"

They'd never called me down to let me know I'd won before, but what else could this be?

"I won!"

"Congratulations. You won. Sort of."

Uh-oh. "Sort of?"

"Actually you tied for first place. You and Patrick, you know, the undertaker's kid."

"Shayla."

"Right, you and Shayla Patrick tied for first."

"I still get the medal, though, right?"

"Sure, both of you will. That's why I needed to see you. We only have one first-place medal on hand for the ceremony, and since you've won two already I'd hoped you wouldn't mind if we gave the actual one we have to Ms. Patrick this afternoon. I promise yours will be here by the end of the week at the latest. Is that all right?"

"So, will my medal say 'tied for first place' or just 'first place'?"

"Other than the year it'll be identical to the last one you won."

"And it will have only my name engraved on the back of it?"

"What'd I just say?"

"OK, I don't mind waiting."

Brown reached his hand across the desk. I leaned forward and shook it.

"Good work," he said, "proud to have you three-peat." He actually almost smiled.

He picked up the phone and pretended he was busy again, letting me know I could leave.

"Oh yeah, Mr. Farrell, I nearly forgot, since no one has ever won the science fair all three of their years at Whittier, we thought we'd surprise you.

"We're pretty sure there's going to be a camera crew

185

from channel twelve and a reporter from the *Journal* at the assembly. They're both trying to do some positive stories on Flint youth and I guess things have gotten so bad that they thought you'd be a good place to start."

"I'ma be in the paper?"

"Seems so."

"And on TV?"

"From what we've heard."

Snap! This would prove to the Sarge how wrong she is about the sucker path. Hard work can get you some good things, you don't always have to scheme and cheat.

He said, "Oh yeah, one last surprise. Your mother might be at the ceremony this afternoon. We called her and she said she was planning on flying out of town and would have to juggle some things but if she could she'd come."

That was even better! She'd have to be right there when I got all my glory!

As I walked back to Ms. Warren's class I tried to be real when I thought about this. Chances were pretty good that the Sarge wouldn't come. She and Darnell Dixon were leaving today for that Adult Foster Care Conference in Washington.

When I walked back into class Ms. Warren said, "From the look on your face I'd have to say that this wasn't the typical visit to the principal's office, Luther."

I was feeling very confident. I looked at Shayla, winked and said, "Sometimes, Ms. Warren, the cards just fall right!"

Shayla looked at me like I was crazy.

I couldn't keep all the cockiness out of my eyes when I

thought, "Oh yeah, baby, I'm crazy all right, crazy in love with you and crazy enough to be the three-peat champion of Flint, Michigan!"

Ah, it's good to see that the universe is still in order. It's got to be reassuring to some folks that the earth is still revolving around the sun, that birds are still flying, that roaches still run when you turn on the light, and that somehow Luther T. Farrell is still always first in line when somebody asks, "Who wants to get their butt royally whipped?"

I didn't even have to look as I followed all the other fools going to the auditorium, I could feel her in the air. I didn't know exactly where the Sarge would be sitting but I knew she was here!

Brown was at the door of the auditorium and pulled me and Shayla and Jeff Sudbury and some seventh-grade girl aside. He led us up on the stage and pointed at four chairs.

Shayla had put her African junk on again this year, you'da thought that might've jinxed her last year but she was as fine and evil as ever. She'd put three beads on each of her locks and was making a clickity-click sound every time her head moved. She'd tucked her locks on the left-hand side behind her ear and even her ear took my breath away.

You know you're in trouble when someone's ears start looking good to you.

If she'd've looked at me I would've smiled and nodded to let her know what Old Man Brown had told me, but she sat with her hands resting in her lap and her eyes closed.

She'd put a dark, dark lipstick on those thick, beautiful

lips. They looked like some kinda luscious living fruit out of the Garden of Eden and, snake or not, baby, I was ready to take a bite. Chester X was right, with this new confidence I was off the hook!

I looked out in the crowd to see where the Sarge was sitting, and there she was, front row, center seat, between Darnell Dixon and Shayla's dad, Mr. Patrick. Shayla's hot mother was sitting next to him, as bad as ever.

Mr. Patrick had on one of his Off to the Graveyard suits and was proud as anything.

Darnell Dixon was bored even before the thing had started. He sat with his legs crossed, his eyes half drooped closed and a toothpick hanging by a hair out of his mouth. He was close enough that I could hear the suck-suck-suck sound he made every few minutes trying to get a piece of something out of one of his back teeth.

And then there was the Sarge.

She was sitting stiff as a board, with one of those just-about-a-smile things on her lips. Our eyes met and I tipped my head at her.

Her eyes rolled.

Whatever.

Brown tapped twice on the microphone and said, "Testing, testing."

All the noise and movement in the auditorium stopped.

"All right, Whittier's mighty Mourning Doves, thank you for that quiet entry. We have both channel twelve and the *Flint Journal* here this afternoon and I know we'll all be proud of the way the world is going to see Whittier Middle School today. Right?

"As you're well aware, this is our fiftieth-annual science fair and a very special one it is. Something that has never occurred in the history of our school is about to happen on this very stage."

He introduced the new judging committee and told all this splah-splah about Whittier Mourning Dove pride and the seriousness of developing new minds, and on and on and on.

Brown finally said, "And now, the awards presentations. But before we begin I'd like to remind everyone not to leave any trash or candy wrappers on the auditorium floor. If you've been wondering why these four students are on the stage it's because they've been volunteered to clean the auditorium afterwards and we hope you'll be considerate."

Big joke. The only one who didn't get it was the seventh grader who was onstage with us. She leaned over to me and whispered, "What? I thought this meant my project won. I ain't cleaning up nothing!"

I guess being around dead people all day makes anything seem funny 'cause about the only person who laughed at Brown's lame joke was Mr. Patrick. He roared like a lion and even gave the Sarge a little nudge with his elbow. But then he looked at her counterfeit smile and her smoking deathly-looking eyes and quit laughing. I bet with the Sarge looking all stiff and unnatural-like that he was afraid that people would think she was a sample of his undertaker work that he'd brought along and propped up beside him to drum up a little business.

Brown nodded at the camerawoman from channel 12. She switched on her bright spotlights as Brown started to give his version of the Let's Pretend the Losers Aren't Losers speech:

". . . very, very difficult to judge . . ."

". . . everyone's a winner here today . . ."

". . . you should all be very proud of what you've done . . ."

Then came the most important word, "However . . ."

"However" or "But" or "Sadly" or even something as whack as "Alas" is the dividing line in all these speeches. If your name comes before the "however" you might as well stand up and get your capital "L" for "loser," 'cause pretty words aside, that's what you are.

Brown kept talking. ". . . So here we go. In third place we are thrilled to give a seventh grader this year's award. Enid Torres, please accept our congratulations and come get your bronze medal."

I don't know if it was the cameras or what, but quite a few people clapped and cheered for the kid. She looked dazzled by the lights and the applause.

Brown shook her hand and gave her the award. The kid leaned into the microphone and said, "Thank you, very much. But we don't have to really clean the auditorium, do we?"

Brown pulled the mike back.

"Next, in second place, taking this year's silver medal, we have Mr. Jeffrey Sudbury. Jeffrey, congratulations on a very strong piece of work, great job."

Jeff strutted over to Brown, got his hand shook and took his award. He leaned into the mike and said, "First I'd like to give all thanks and all glory to my savior, Jesus Christ, 'cause without his help and love I wouldn'ta been able to stomp all you losers. Then I'd like to dedicate this to my moms. Moms, you been there for me from the beginning and this is all because of you. Then I want to give a shout-out to all my dogs from the south side, Too-Too, Bay-Bay—"

Brown grabbed the mike back.

"I'm sure Mr. Too and Mr. Bay will be happy to accept your thanks later, Sudbury. Take a seat.

"Finally," Brown said, "history is about to be made. And in honor of this history we have invited the special parents of two special students to join us today. First, two of Flint's most outstanding citizens, Harrison and Saundra Patrick."

Shayla's mom and dad stood up and waved. From looking at her mom it was easy to see why Shayla was so fine. Good thing, too, 'cause it was real obvious that Mr. Patrick's genes needed some serious neutralizing.

"And," Brown said, "one of our community's busiest and most successful businesswomen, Ms. Carol Farrell."

The Sarge didn't move, no standing and waving for her.

Shayla still had her eyes closed and her hands folded in her lap. Those Garden of Eden lips were moving just the littlest bit, you'd have to be paying real close attention to notice and that's just what I was doing.

When things are going your way you kind of look at what's really important, you don't want to get knocked out of your mood by thinking about any kind of nonsense. That's why the only thing I was thinking about was Shayla Patrick. But I guess philosophy must be real important to me too, because I was thinking in a very philosophical way about the time that me and Shayla had spent together.

I knew I'd done a lot of things wrong to her, right from the minute I'd first met her and I'd stole a kiss off her kneecap. Chester X had been right, I oughta apologize or explain for the stupid, mean things I'd said to her for all these years and how I hadn't been honest about the way I feel for her. I knew I oughta —

"Actually," Brown said, "two pieces of history are about to be made today. One is that for the first time in the fair's fifty years we have a tie for first place in the science fair!"

Eloise Exum screamed, "Yes! I told you you were gonna win, girl!"

Sparky yelled, "That's my boy!"

I stared at Shayla. She took a deep breath, opened her eyes and smiled at me!

I smiled back and stuck my hand out to her.

The Garden of Eden lips spread even more and she showed those teeth that I'd once told her looked like a row of tombstones. She reached both of her hands out and squeezed mine!

If I was about to die this wouldn't exactly be my last request, but like I said, I like to keep it real, and this was close enough for me right now! Besides, I've had lots of practice improving these kinds of times in my fantasies.

Brown said, "Ms. Shayla Patrick, it gives me such pleasure to award you first place in this year's science fair!"

Shayla pulled away from my hand and clickety-clicked, clickety-clicked over to Brown.

I noticed a wonderful smell and brought my hand to my nose. This was too much. Shayla was wearing some real classy African perfume, I think it's called Jungle Gardenia.

Brown said, "Since the winning entries were both such works of art this year we've decided to do something different to honor them. Lucas."

Lucas Sorge knew his computers. The lights on the stage dimmed and a screen dropped down behind us.

Brown said, "Lucas and Mr. Cho have put together a special PowerPoint presentation detailing your winning projects. And we have given each of your parents a DVD copy to cherish forever!"

It's too bad Lucas had already made this little flick, it would be a lot more interesting if it showed how the Sarge reacted to my winning. Her heart must be getting ready to bust from jealousy because I was showing her that her philosophy didn't work, that mine was what was important. This was probably the most bitter moment of her long bitter life!

They showed Shayla's project first. It started with a shot of Shayla laughing and covering her mouth with her hand in slow motion. Lucas made the film so good that you'da thought Spike Lee had put it all together. And there she was on the big screen, my Nubian goddess, Shayla Patrick, profiling like a movie queen.

There was music in the background and interviews with teachers and students telling how smart and charming Shayla was. And that was nothing but the truth.

Her project was called "What Is Cellular Differentiation and What Are the Mechanisms Responsible for It?" I know, boring. But her and her dad had hired the same geniuses they'd hired last year and it was very sharp.

As I sat watching Shayla's project and all the work

she'd put into it I couldn't help but feel proud and amazed that I'd actually tied with her. You know, the girl was beautiful *and* smart, kind of like a female version of me.

Lucas ended the presentation with a picture of my sweet Shayla smiling softly, kinda like she was thinking, "Oh, Luther! You are so funny!"

The whole auditorium applauded and gave Shayla much respect when the music ended and the stage lights came back on. Then the lights went back out and a giant picture of my head came up on the screen. Laughs and disrespect flowed through the crowd like blood pumping through your aorta.

Aw, no. This can't be happening!

I *know* I look a lot better than how Lucas's camera was showing me. That little clown had gone and digitally put a couple thousand more pimples on my face!

Mr. Cho narrated the piece. "Lead poisoning," he started, "one of those problems from the early to mid-twentieth century that we thought was a part of our past, but a problem whose legacy continues to plague us.

"Normally a ninth grader isn't what you think of when you mention the word 'crusader,' but that's precisely what Flint, Michigan's, Whittier Middle School student Luther T. Farrell has turned out to be."

Like a bug's eyes are drawn to a spider's fangs I looked over at the Sarge. Her expression never changed, but her eyes slowly dropped from the screen and locked in on me. The cockiness that Mr. X had warned me about was all over my face, and that's right where I wanted it to be.

Mr. Cho's voice kept going. "Luther has combined the

194

traditional science fair project with some top-rate investigative journalism and detective work to expose a horrible fact of life in twenty-first century Flint, Michigan; the continued, criminal plague of leaded paint in many of our inner-city homes and apartments . . ."

Branded moments.

One second I was looking the Sarge dead in her eye, kinda nodding my head up and down like I was saying all over again, "Oh yeah, how you like me now," and the next second all the sounds and lights and even the oxygen in the auditorium went away with a giant swoosh!

I swear to God that that was the first time it hit me. Not in all the months I'd been working on my project, not in all the books I'd read, not in all the Web sites I'd visited, not with all the people I'd interviewed had I ever put one and one together and seen what I was doing.

That's when it felt like another tile had jumped offa Taco Bell and smacked me right upside my head. That was the first time that my mind let me see what the basement of the house on Fourth Street was jammed with: about two hundred million gallons of stale leaded paint!

Darnell had told me that right after the government made leaded paint illegal a long time ago the Sarge had printed up some cards that said she was a paint disposal expert and had gone around to all the paint stores she could find and offered to get rid of their paint for a small fee.

And that's what she'd been doing ever since, getting rid of the paint one gallon at a time on her houses and apartments.

Cho kept talking. "Through the clever use of archival

footage, his project shows in heartbreaking detail the ad-verse effects of lead on the development of growing chil-dren."

The Sarge's expression was growing hotter and hotter.

Cho kept reading. "And here's a surprise for young Mr. Farrell, the selection committee thought his project was so well done and so timely that they actually notified both the city manager's and the mayor's offices. It's now my distinct pleasure to introduce the mayor, the honorable Richard Banks. Mayor Banks."

The mayor came from backstage and pulled some notes out of his jacket pocket.

"Fellow citizens, it is with the greatest pride that I an-nounce that my administration will aggressively work to look after the needs of the citizens of our wonderful city and will put an end to this problem."

My science fair project was going to end up costing the Sarge a ton of cash or maybe even some time in jail!

The mayor turned around and looked at me. "Mr. Farrell, thank you for your great work. And while my ad-ministration has been working on this for quite a while we are grateful that a young citizen did care enough to reach some of the same conclusions that we will be releasing in a report very soon.

"Luther T. Farrell," he said, "you have pushed this ad-ministration to do some very positive things and I have pushed the state legislature to promise that the allocation for inspection of lead painted housing in Flint will be tripled next year!"

People clapped.

The mayor said, "I've also instructed the prosecutor's office to investigate what charges we can lay against the irresponsible, criminal landlords who have perpetrated this injustice on our youngest citizens."

They might as well have tied me to a tree and said, "Ready, aim, fire!" Lucas had made the final shot of the film a clip of a little girl suffering from severe lead poisoning. She was trembling and making a sound like a Siamese cat that just got its tail cut off.

I didn't even have to watch the screen, I could see the look of horror on the faces of everyone in the audience.

That genius Lucas Sorge had even put a reverb sound on the girl's cry and it echoed through the auditorium, sounding like death itself, finally fading into a blood-bubbling silence.

The Sarge's coffin smile never left her face but both of her eyebrows slowly arched at the same time! Wow! I'd *never* seen that before. All I could think of was that book Ms. Warren had made us read and the only line I could remember from it, "Ahh, and what fresh Hell is this?"

Even Darnell Dixon was paying attention now. His toothpick was pointed at me like a little arrow, and he was sucking on the piece of food jammed in his teeth so hard and fast that his mouth sounded like one of those Cartoon Network time bombs getting ready to blow. He was going "tickticktick-tickticktick!"

Darnell smiled and mouthed something in my direction. I can't be sure. I think it was "You're mine this time, fool."

The newswoman from channel 12 gave me the thumbs-up sign and the reporter from the *Journal* was nodding and writing real quick in his notebook. I could see tomorrow's headlines: "FORMERLY CONFIDENT, HANDSOME YOUNG GENIUS FINDS TRUE LOVE AND WINS THREE-PEAT THE DAY BEFORE HE DISAPPEARS—FOUL PLAY SUSPECTED. PSYCHO MOTHER QUESTIONED."

Brown shook my hand and gave me an empty rectangular box. If that wasn't symbolic of a coffin I don't know what is.

The adults in the audience started clapping and actually stood up! Most of the students did too, my first and last standing ovation all rolled into one!

It was almost like they knew this was about to be the final scene in the life and times of Luther T. Farrell. I looked at everybody standing and cheering for my project and thought, even though I wasn't really ready to die, "I bet not even the most expensive package at the House of Patrick Mortuary would've been a nicer send-off."

· 15 ·

LUTHER'S LONG LAST LIMO RIDE

The *Journal* and channel 12 both interviewed me. I couldn't believe how cool I was acting, I was saying mature junk like ". . . children growing without the added problems of developmental difficulties caused by lead exposure . . ." and ". . . no, I don't really have any plans to go into politics, I'm just trying to do my best to help point out problems in the community. I'm just one of the little people doing the best he can."

I think one time I even put my hand on my chin, stroked where the six little cat hairs used to be, wrinkled my brow and was nodding my head up and down.

It was like having the camera on you turned you into a genius! I wonder if a lot of those politicians and business folks and newspeople you see on TV are just as messed up as me in real life and only sound smart when the camera is on them.

A little line of people started coming up onstage to shake the winners' hands.

Ms. Warren was first, she actually gave me a big hug and a kiss on the cheek! I guess she was so blown away by my project that she just said forget the zero tolerance on touching students rule.

She squeezed my hand and said, "I am so proud of you. But I've known you were special from day one."

Then Old Lady Scott said, "Well, Luther, you really did deserve to win *this* time."

Like she had to rub in the fact that I'd beaten her girl last year.

Then Mr. Moliassi from eighth grade: "Luther, I am shocked at the quality and depth of your work."

Like he wouldn't've been any more amazed if he found out that chimpanzees had designed the space shuttle.

Then Coach Williams said, "You know, Farrell, after seeing you play basketball I just knew there had to be something that you were halfway good at."

So what if I can't dribble? Besides, who wants to be good at something that's called dribbling?

Then Mr. and Mrs. Patrick smiled at me and shook my hand.

He said, "Luther, you've got to stop by for dinner someday. You and Shayla have been friends for years and we don't see enough of you."

I thought, "Don't worry, Mr. Patrick, you're gonna be seeing a whole lot more of me soon, just wait until Darnell Dixon is done."

Then I heard that Road Runner time bomb getting

ready to blow. I don't know what it was that was stuck in Darnell's back tooth but he was going at it so tough that it seemed like if he didn't ease up he'd be the first person to perform a root canal on himself.

I hadn't seen the sadistic dog smile so big and real since he'd broke that dude's fingers.

He slapped me on the back. Hard!

"My man! You really outdid yourself this time! Pointing out the dangers of leaded paint! Hoo-hoo! You're gonna have to give me a private demonstration of your project. You watch, once I get back from D.C., you and me are gonna have a real deep discussion about what you done."

He walked past me laughing.

I looked at who was next in line and wished I hadn't.

The Sarge didn't even look in my eyes. Her brows were both still arched way up on her forehead like someone had braided her hair so tight that it had lifted her eyebrows three inches.

She pretended she was fiddling around with something on my collar, then leaned in and pretended she was kissing my cheek.

She whispered, and it couldn't've come through any clearer if she'd've shouted: "Oh yeah, hotshot, so I'm gonna surmise that you've already given consideration to the consequences. I'm gonna postulate that you've already made other living arrangements.

"Consider this your four days' notice, that's how long I'm gonna be gone. You keep your eye on my clients until I'm back, then you know what to do. Have everything ready to roll. Don't take anything that's not yours, which pretty much limits you to some clothes, some CDs, that private journal and those magazines you've got hidden under your mattress. Need I say more?"

I hated myself for answering, "No, ma'am."

She squeezed my cheeks, smiled that death's door grin and said loud enough for folks to hear, "You little dickens you, who else but you could do something like this? I can't wait to get back from Washington so we can do something extra special to celebrate! You spend the next four days thinking about what it is you deserve and I promise you I'll be doing the same thing."

People actually smiled at this death threat, everyone but Mr. Patrick. He was staring at the Sarge, giving her a look like he knew there was something very wrong going on here but he just couldn't figure out what it was.

Finally Shayla's drop-dead gorgeous mom pulled him away by his arm and hissed, "Harrison! What is wrong with you?"

Things got seriously blurred after that. What had I been thinking? I know how luck runs in the life and times of Luther T. Farrell, I should've known something as messed up as this would happen and I'd end up being homeless or living with Sparky and his crazy family. But even that was wishful thinking, I knew the Sarge was gonna sic Darnell Dixon on me and after that *living* in itself would be a great accomplishment.

The Sarge always said she could tolerate just about anything except someone messing with her pocketbook and I'd gone *way* past messing. My three-peat science fair project, Yes!, was gonna cost her big-time.

I don't know exactly what a great philosopher would say about this, but it seemed even to me like I'd gone way out of my way to sabotage the Sarge, and I swear that that wasn't what I'd meant to do.

I sleepwalked through the next half hour. I got patted on the back and hand-shooked a lot more times and still couldn't stop wondering why I'd done something so stupid just to get that three-peat, Wahoo!, in a science fair?

But it was four days before payback time, and three gold medals, Hey, hey hey!, hanging on the wall might not be a real good price to pay for what was about to happen to me.

What am I talking about, ". . . three gold medals hanging on the wall . . ."? More like three gold medals rattling around in a cardboard box with my clothes, my CDs, my journal and my under-the-mattress magazine collection.

How did she know about those magazines? It's a good thing I've had lots of practice being humiliated, that's another shot that an inexperienced or nonphilosophical person would've fell apart after.

The crowd started thinning out and I saw Shayla and her parents heading toward the door. I guess now was the time to follow Chester X's plan. I guess there wouldn't be any other time to tell her that I loved and respected her even though I couldn't keep myself from talking to her like a dog.

Before I could get to her the reporter from the *Journal* grabbed me again.

"Luther, I just need to check some details."

When the *Journal* was done with me Shayla and her family had disappeared so I decided to head home and start packing.

I'd just gotten through the doors of the auditorium when the hair on my neck started tingling. I heard the sucksucksuck of Darnell's jammed food.

He came up behind me and said, "Here you go, sport."

He reached the weekly receipts briefcase toward me.

"Your moms says this here is time-sensitive and since we spent time at this lovely little ceremony we aren't going to be able to get to the bank. You've gotta take care of this today, you know what goes where."

I took the briefcase from Darnell.

He stuck his empty hand out in my direction.

"Hand 'em over, sport."

"What?"

"The keys to the ride. Your moms says you can call taxis for the Crew tomorrow morning. Welcome to the World of the Walking, my brother."

"How'm I supposed to get home?" I was already twisting the bus's keys off my ring.

"Well, sport, the way I see it you've got two options. Either call some of your new homies from the mayor's office or wait here for a while and I'll send your old friend Patton Turner over to get you."

Darnell took the two keys I handed him, then snatched my key ring away from me before I could get it back in my pocket.

"Hey!" I said. "She told me I had four days before I had to get out."

Darnell called himself imitating me but he whined way too much and my voice has never been that high, even before I had these major hormones surging through my veins. "'Boo-hoo. She told me I had four days before I had to get out!'

"Relax, chump, I'm not taking the house keys from you, I'm just checking to make sure you don't have any copies of your ride's keys on here. I'm parking it at the home and I believe her orders were that you weren't even to *think* about looking at it."

What kind of an idiot would think you'd make duplicate keys, then leave them on the same key ring as the originals?

I didn't say a word. He threw my keys on the floor, then stuck his hand out again.

I said, "What? I don't have any duplicate keys." On the same ring, fool, but I know where the Sarge keeps them at the home.

He said, "The medal. She said since she supplied the paint that won that award it only seems right that the medal is hers too."

"All they gave me was an empty box, I'm supposed to get the medal later."

He snatched the box out of my hand, shook it twice, then threw it on the floor.

He stuck his hand out again.

I said, "I swear, Shayla got the only medal, mine's coming later." My voice really was sounding high-pitched and whiny.

He said, "Wallet."

He didn't think I was just going to hand over my wallet, did he? You can only push a man so far before something snaps in him.

I don't know how it happened but the next thing I knew, there my hand was, putting my wallet in Darnell Dixon's hand.

He pulled out all my credit cards and my fifty-dollar emergency money and tucked them in his front pocket.

He got ready to throw the wallet on the floor but said, "What's this?" He ran his fingers over the zero on my wallet.

Oh no! No! Not Chauncey!

He laughed and ripped Chauncey's package open and exposed him to the air.

I think the scientific word for what had happened to Chauncey is called vulcanization. He was powdery and stiff and you could tell there was no way he'd ever be unrolled. If this had been on the Cartoon Channel little moths would've been flying out.

Darnell shot Chauncey down the hall like he was a flour-coated rubber band.

He said, "Don't worry, sport. Let me go out to your momma's car for a second, she just bought three dozen of 'em for our trip to Washington. Maybe I can let you borrow one."

This was so weak that I didn't even have to think "Your words cannot harm me, my mind is like a shield of steel."

But it did come to mind.

What else came to mind was that Darnell was completely off the leash now. All the years that he'd been patiently waiting to get me were finally paying off.

He tossed my wallet down next to the keys and the empty first prize, Yes!, box and poor Chauncey's wrapper and left. Good thing, too, I was about this far from putting some respect in him.

I didn't trust myself not to go off if I saw the Sarge in the parking lot so I went around to the front door of the school. I had a good half-hour walk ahead of me.

Things were bad. The Sarge had called me a dickens and Darnell kept calling me sport. There's no way that either one of these things could be called a good omen.

The sound of a car's horn ripped through the air and my heart.

I whipped around expecting to see the Sarge's Benz barreling down on me but it was a big black Cadillac limousine.

The passenger's window whizzed down and Shayla's mom said, "I can't believe the Three-peat Kid is walking home. You deserve a limo ride. Hop in back."

Shayla's dad said, "Hold on for a second, Luther."

He looked in the backseat and said, "Shayla, carefully slide Mr. Ramirez over to the other seat, his viewing isn't until five and I don't want to have his embalming fluid settle in one place before then."

I think this is supposed to be what they call gallows humor.

Mrs. Patrick said, "You couldn't possibly imagine what we have to go through every day, Luther."

I gave a weak laugh.

The back door opened and the clickety-click of beads rolled out of the car as Shayla slid over to make room for me.

I stuck my head in and looked all around the back of

the limo. I mean sure, it seemed like Shayla's dad was joking, but what if he wasn't? You never know how weird some people might be. I didn't need any more drama in my life and if I had to bump around in the backseat with a corpse I'd rather walk.

There were no Ramirezes in there.

I got in.

Well, if nothing else good happened on this trip at least the seat was still warm from Shayla sitting there!

The divider window between the front seat of the car and the backseat started up. Shayla rolled her eyes and said, "No need, Daddy."

We drove along not talking for a while, her looking out the left window and me looking out the right.

Finally I said, "Hey, Shayla."

She said, "Hey."

I said, "Congratulations, your project was bad."

She looked at me for the first time since I got in.

She said, "Thank you," turned her head back to look out the window, then whipped it right back around to look at me. "But you know what?" she said. "I've decided I'm not gonna allow myself to feel the least bit guilty. I'm just going to look at this as us finally being even."

"Huh?"

She said, "You know what I mean. Your project was great, Luther. You showed much more imagination and initiative than I ever did. You should've won the gold this year. I should've won the gold last year, so I guess that makes us close to being even."

This was another one of those branded moments, but

this was one of those rare good ones! Between the warm seat and that comment, this ride home in a hearse was something I'd be remembering till the end of my life, or for the next four days, which were close to being the same thing.

I was doubly surprised, first because Shayla was out-and-out giving me much respect, and second because it seemed so important to me, it seemed like it made me glow!

Now was my big chance to let her know what my heart was really feeling. Finally I was going to be able to tell her what I'd been practicing on since Mr. X said I should.

I said, "Yeah. Whatever."

She rolled her eyes again and looked back out the left window. I looked back out the right. I saw my reflection in the glass and got the third surprise of my ride in the Death Mobile. Here I was, pretty much a walking dead man, but I was grinning like the biggest fool in the world!

· 16 ·

BUCKING THE SARGE

After the Munster Mobile let me off at the home I peeked through the window of the dayroom. Cool! Everyone was watching TV and no one had their noses plugged. After I checked on the Crew I headed down to my room.

Chester X was reading the newspaper.

"Hey, Mr. X."

"Well, did you do it, did you win again? By that expression I'd say someone lobbed another grenade at Luther T. Farrell's confidence."

"No, Mr. X, it went good. I won the three-peat, but I tied with Shayla Patrick."

"Great! Are we going to have a special ceremony to hang that third medal?"

"I won't get it until tomorrow at the earliest."

"That's why you're looking so down?"

"No. The Sarge found out what my project was on and gave me my four days' notice."

"Your what?"

"My four days' notice. I got until she gets back from Washington to pack my stuff."

"Mercy! That's gotta be some kind of record, I don't believe I've ever heard of anything less than two weeks' notice before, on anything."

Mr. X started counting off on his fingers. "Not on getting fired, not on getting evicted, not on even getting axed by your woman, usually you get a lot more time than that. No, four days is surely some kind of record."

"Well, I got a plan. I don't want you to get your hopes up but I think you might be involved."

"Really? You aren't thinking about . . ." From the tone of his voice you could hear his hopes rising.

"Like I said, Mr. X, I've got to do some investigating before I say anything."

"Luther," he said, "you don't get to be my age by being impatient. I know you're going to do the right thing! I knew you were too smart to take this forever. And don't you think for a minute that I don't know what would happen if I was in this home without you looking over me."

I ignored his try to make me feel guilty. "Mr. X, after what I did I don't think 'smart' and the name Luther T. Farrell belong in the same sentence."

"Well, how 'bout a hand of tunk? Maybe if I take some of your money from you it'll help you forget your problems."

"Thanks, but I've got to get all this stuff"—I patted the weekly receipts briefcase—"into the bank before it closes. I'm gonna try and find where she's got my education fund, maybe it's in something that I can withdraw right away."

"Don't you forget, son, I've got a little salted away myself. We can live pretty good for a while on that if we're careful. I can get a job and with all those gorgeous Florida women and their naturally generous Southern nature you'll be rolling in dough."

I said, "If I've been figuring right I should have at least ninety grand in that account, Mr. X, I think I'll be OK."

"You keep me and my little savings in mind anyway."

The phone rang.

Mr. Foster opened the basement door and yelled down, "Luther, it's your mom and she doesn't sound too happy."

Uh-oh.

I picked up the phone. "Hello?"

"What are you still doing there?"

I said, "You said I've got four days, who am I supposed to get to look after the Crew if I leave now?"

"You know what I mean. Don't you play dumb with me, Mr. Lead Crusader. You'd *better* be there through Monday. I'm talking about why aren't you at the bank making those deposits?"

"How'm I supposed to get there? Darnell took my keys and my money."

"Use petty cash and take a cab. Listen," she said, "I'm calling from the plane. Something told me to call and make sure you got those deposits in. Don't jerk me around on this, it's very important you get them to Elaine before the bank closes. I could lose some houses if this isn't done in time. Need I say more?"

I couldn't believe she'd waste money on a plane phone call to remind me to do something I'd been doing for years. And those calls cost about a hundred dollars a minute! But maybe she'd gotten nervous thinking that I'd get revenge on her by deliberately not putting the deposits in.

Hmmm!

I took too long to answer her.

She yelled, which she almost never does, "Need I say more!"

I yelled back, "No!"

"OK," she said, her usual calm, Darth Vader voice coming back, "OK, I see that your testosterone level has gotten so high that you're man enough to shout at *me*, huh? Let me tell you something, you'd better pray that these next four days do something to mellow me out because if they don't, may God have mercy on your soul."

She slammed the phone down so hard that I bet the plane's pilot had to make an announcement about unexpected turbulence and turn on the Fasten Seat Belts sign. I bet a air marshal jumped up with his gun drawn.

I headed up to the office.

Who did she think she was talking to? It's a good thing she was on that plane because if she was anywhere within thirty miles of Flint I'd hunt her down and lay some real serious pain on her and her little rent-a-thug.

I opened all three of the office's locks and went in to get

the petty cash and the safety deposit key. The key and the petty cash were kept in a Bible inside her desk drawer. She'd always said that if you wanted to hide something from a thief all you had to do was put it in a book, especially a Bible, so she'd had me take a razor blade and hollow out a little secret compartment. I'd sliced out all the way from Genesis to the first parts of Revelations.

I was so mad I snatched at the drawer where she kept the hollow Bible and it flew across the room like a Frisbee. The drawer landed upside down on the floor.

There was a piece of duct tape pressed to the bottom of the drawer. I peeled it back and there was the safety deposit key, stuck in the tape.

This was strange. She forgot to tell me she'd moved the key's hiding place. So if it hadn't been for my little temper tantrum how'd she figure I'd get into the safety deposit box?

Maybe I'd just pretend I didn't find it and couldn't make those deposits, then we'd see how old Miss Never Make a Mistake liked that.

I turned the drawer over and started putting back all the things that had fallen out.

When I picked up the Bible and took the cash out, there the safety deposit key was in its usual place.

Hmmm, the one that was in the duct tape was probably a spare. I taped the spare key back under the drawer and put the regular one in my pocket.

I got all the Sarge's other junk back in the drawer and slid it into the desk.

That's when it hit me. I may be slow, but if you give me enough time I'll figure most things out.

I took the safety deposit key out of my pocket and looked at the number on the top, R 581.

I pulled the drawer completely out, untaped the key and looked at its number, V 441.

I stood there staring at the keys. This other key could only mean that the Sarge had another safety deposit box that was so secret she even kept it from me!

I always thought that there were whole tons of records that I hadn't seen and here they were. This secret safety deposit box was probably where she kept my education fund deposit book.

I couldn't believe it. Not that she had other records— she's always keeping track of anything that has to do with her money. If there was a way she could get a tax deduction out of it I bet she'd've kept track of how many times Mr. Baker farted in 2002.

What was hard to believe was that she'd be so sloppy that I'd find out where she was keeping these records. Maybe she *was* softening up in her old age. Too bad I wasn't going to be around to check out the New Improved Compassionate Sarge.

I put both keys in my pocket and slid the drawer back. I picked up the weekly receipts briefcase and redid all three office locks.

It looked like my visit to the bank might be more interesting than I thought.

The cab let me off in front of the bank. As soon as I got in I headed over to the office that had Elaine Jones, Personal Investments Counselor written on the door.

She was looking at a computer screen when I knocked. She smiled. "Luther, how are you today?"

"I'm fine, thanks, Elaine."

She went to a safe and got the bank's key for the safety deposit box. I followed her to a vault and we both put our keys in door number V 581. She slid the drawer out and walked it over to a privacy booth.

She started to close the booth's door.

"Thanks, Elaine."

"You're quite welcome. If there's anything you need, let me know."

"OK."

When she'd closed the door I took all of the Sarge's log-books and receipt records and put them in their proper folders and logged what I'd done. I got the deposit slips written out for Elaine and closed the box back up.

"I'm all done." I handed her the slips and the cash.

"Great. Let me get my key, and we'll see you next week, Luther."

Not unless you're planning on visiting the Patrick House of Mortuary.

I slapped my head just like I'd practiced and said, "Ooh! I almost forgot, she wanted me to get into the other box too." I reached the secret key toward her and held my breath.

"Oh." She took the key from my hand. "It's over in the rollaways, I'm going to need your help, Luther."

"Sure."

We headed into an area that only had five or six storage boxes. They were all on wheels and the size of the safes that you see in the cartoons.

"We'll take it into there, Luther, the B room."

I got behind the box and started pushing it.

Elaine said, "Wow, Luther, you're quite strong. It usually takes me and Mr. Dixon both to move this one."

Darnell! It seemed like I was the only one that this secret box was a secret to.

"Uh, yeah, I guess I am. I've been hitting the weights a little lately."

We horsed the box into the room.

"Thanks, Elaine."

I closed the door and held my breath. I don't know why but my hands were actually shaking as I put my key in next to the one that Elaine had put in.

I took a deep breath and opened the safety deposit safe's door.

No poisonous gas, no genie of death, not even a corpse that the Sarge and Darnell were waiting to ditch once the coast was clear.

Just a pile of folders, some bankbooks, a metal box and a bunch of the same ledger books that she had me make entries in every week.

I started with the metal box.

Bingo! It had a little over $50,000 in fifties and hundreds, and they looked and felt real. I put them back in the exact same order I'd found them.

Then I started with the folder on top.

Inside it were the titles to the Sarge's Benz, the pickup

truck, the cube van, the snowplow and a certain brand-new white-on-white-in-white Riviera, along with the power of attorney forms she'd signed over to me. I could understand the Benz, the pickup, the cube van and the plow, but Darnell's Rivy Dog?

When I saw that the title was in the Sarge's name it all got clear. No wonder Darnell Dixon was making minimum wage but could afford a new Riviera every two years, she was buying them for him!

I couldn't believe it! But maybe this was part of some deal they'd worked out, maybe it was like me getting all my wages put in the education fund instead of in my hand.

The next folder had FNL written on it. I could tell from the columns and numbers inside that that stood for Friendly Neighbor Loans. The names of the people who'd borrowed money were all in initials, but I could figure a lot of them out.

Next to the names of the people who'd had problems repaying their loans in what the Sarge called a timely fashion were the initials D.D. These had to be the poor broke-fingered, banged-up-kneecapped, bloody-nosed folks that she'd turned over to the Darnell Dixon "I Bet Your Trifling Soul Won't Be Late Again" Collection Agency.

Two lines in the ledger were highlighted in yellow. One was from a couple years ago and had the initials P.T. and the number 1500, and the other one was dated from exactly a year ago and had the initials B.S. and the number 1700 written next to it. In a red pen the word FORGIVEN was written through both of the lines.

B.S. had originally borrowed $1200 but had let the interest run it up to $1700.

So this was how much my victory in last year's science fair had cost. B.S. had to be Ms. Scott, she was on the hook to the Sarge. The Sarge had stole the science fair results by letting Ms. Scott not pay her loan back. I felt like I'd been gut-punched.

No wonder I was nervous about opening this box. The P.T. must've been for Peter Thompson, the guy from the Secretary of State's office.

The next three folders had the deeds to what looked like fifty houses in Flint. The first folder had ACTIVE printed across the front of it. Inside were all the houses that she was still collecting payments for.

The second folder had a big X written across the front. Inside of it were all the houses that she'd let go for taxes or that the city had demolished, including Marcel Marx and Poofy's house.

The next folder had the deeds to the three group homes.

The next folder had D.D. in big blue letters across the front of it. Inside were the deeds to ten or eleven houses. I peeped out what was happening real quick from the addresses. At least six of them were the houses that Mr. Baker, the Human Torch, had been transferred to. And all of them had gone up in flames.

I restacked the folders just like they'd been when I took them out. No need for the Sarge to know I'd busted her.

I started riffling through her bankbooks, trying to keep

a running total of the balances. It's funny how a couple of twenty thousands here and a couple of forty thousands there add up real quick. I finally lost track. I couldn't believe how much money she had off the books. I couldn't believe how cheap she was being with my crew, with all the other aides and with me.

The last bankbook made me get all nervous again. My education fund.

I picked it up and pulled the book out of the little envelope it was in. That was a good sign, at least it was still in my name.

On the first line of the first page was the original $900 deposit we'd made together on my twelfth birthday. On the second line of the first page was absolutely nothing. A sad story that repeated itself all the way to the end of the book.

$900.

Years of all those hours for $900. That probably worked out to about a penny an hour.

I stood there holding the stupid book.

I thought about what the Sarge had told me once about ideas and language, about how if an idea was clearly thought out and well reasoned the words you needed to express that idea came to you real easy and plain. You didn't have to do any fumbling around to find words to describe what you were thinking, they just came.

What was happening to me now was a lot like that. I had a problem and the solution to that problem came to me as clear as anything. Everything I needed to do was just there, like I'd been thinking about it for years, not for just the few seconds since, surprise!, I'd seen the nearly empty education fund bankbook.

Just like that I knew everything I had to do.

I could feel all my worries lift off my back. Instead of putting all the Sarge's folders back in the safety deposit vault I put them in the weekly receipt briefcase along with my education-fund bankbook and the $50,000 that'd been floating around.

The Sarge and Darnell had better be ready, they weren't the only ones who had four days to plot revenge. If they thought Luther T. Farrell was going to roll over and play dead they had another thought coming.

A great philosopher, whose name escapes me at the moment, once said, "Revenge is a dish best served cold." And I was about to get seriously chilly on the Sarge and Darnell Dixon.

17

ANOTHER MEDIA CONSPIRACY
AGAINST A YOUNG BRUH

When six o'clock came I told the Crew, "OK, gentlemen, we've got to turn the cartoons off for a minute, you're going to get a chance to see your favorite health care professional on the news."

Mr. Foster said, "I wouldn't get so excited, Luther, finding yourself on the six o'clock news usually isn't a real positive thing for a young black man."

"Maybe not, but you might get excited when you see what a genius some people think this young black man is."

"Luther," Mr. Foster said, "there's no way possible for you to be more of a genius in my eyes than you already are."

Mr. Baker said, "You mean we don't get to watch *Teamo Supremo* just 'cause you're trying to be a genius?"

I told him, "Don't worry, Mr. Baker, it should only be a few minutes, it'll probably be the first story."

None of them looked too happy.

The newspeople always liked to tease you before they went to the first set of commercials, and the anchorwoman said, "Tragedy strikes on Dayton Street. A happy reunion, maybe? School cuts worse than predicted, and a no-go on that new truck. This is Karen Russell with all the news that matters plus the first in a new series on the positive things some of our local youths have been up to along with Flint's most accurate, up-to-date weather and sports reports coming up next on *TV Twelve News*."

The first story wasn't me. The reporter said, "Flint is on pace for a record year in homicides as three bodies were discovered in this abandoned North End house . . . bla, bla, bla."

The next couple of stories weren't me either.

After the first bunch of commercials Mr. Baker said, "Where were you? Did we miss you, Mr. Big-Shot Genius?"

"Just hold on, they like to get the bad news out of the way first."

With this being Flint I should've known they'd have about twenty more minutes of bad news to get out of the way, but this was ridiculous. It was already 6:29.

Maybe there was going to be a special report on the science fair, maybe they were going to delay the national news to show the report on me.

When they finally quit showing commercials the main newswoman said, "And finally, in this, our first in a series on the good things Flint teens have been up to, fifteen-year-old Loser T.—"

Oh no! No she didn't!

She laughed and looked down on her desk. "I'm sorry,

that's fifteen-year-old *Luther* T. Farrell set an impressive record at Whittier Middle School this afternoon. Our reporter Joyce Morgan was there to record the happy event."

The woman who'd interviewed me said, "That's right, Karen, Luther and his fifteen-year-old classmate, Shayla Patrick, tied for first place at the fiftieth-annual Whittier Middle School science fair this afternoon. For Luther this was his third win in a row, and that has never before been done at this south-side Flint school.

"I had the chance to talk to young Mr. Farrell about his accomplishment."

The TV showed a picture of the auditorium, then a close-up on me.

I couldn't believe how bad I looked. I kept sticking my tongue out and licking my lips and I was blinking like someone had poured salt in my eyes. When my eyes were opened they were staring right into the camera like I was hypnotized. It also looked like Lucas Sorge had gone and digitally put a bunch more pimples on my face. You could even see me taking giant breaths like I just ran five miles!

Mr. Baker said, "Gee, Luther, that's just how you look when you know your mom is on her way over!"

I gave him a dirty look.

But maybe when they heard my answers to her questions I'd end up looking a little better. The reporter said, "Luther, I know your project was about the dangers of lead in paint. Great job, how does it feel to get the three-peat?"

I blinked like I was sending out some secret code with my eyes and licked my lips like a thirsty dog going after a bowl of water, then said, "Uh . . . it feels, like, real good, I guess."

She said, "So does this mean we have a future great scientist in our midst?"

Lick, lick, lick. Blink, blink, blink. "Uh . . . I guess so."

She said, "I imagine you and your parents are going to have a big celebration tonight."

Blink, blink, blink. Lick, lick, lick. "Uh . . . uh-huh."

The camera came back to a live shot of her. She said, "So that's it. Just one of the positive things that Flint's teenagers are up to. This is Joyce Morgan at Whittier Middle School."

The anchorwoman, Karen Russell, said, "Great report, Joyce. And congratulations to those two winners, I apologize for blowing your name, Luther, as we can see you are definitely not a loser."

Then that ignorant joking weatherman who's never funny and never right about the weather said, "I think we can forgive you on that one, Karen. After all, 'Luther' is how you'd say 'loser' if you had a lisp, right?" He tapped his pencil on the desk and gave a sappy grin while the anchorpeople and the sports idiot groaned and laughed.

Karen Russell said, "And on that note, it's time for Peter Jennings and ABC *World News Tonight*. Thank you once again for joining Flint's number one . . ."

The whole crew was looking at me real sympathetic.

I said, "What?"

Mr. Baker hit the remote back to the Cartoon Network. He mumbled, "I can't believe we missed *Teamo Supremo* to watch you squirm like a worm in a skillet, Luther. We can see that same kind of performance any day. Only difference is we get to see it live."

What could I say? I was in a state of shock. They'd cut out all the good questions and my real intelligent answers to make me look like a complete fool.

But why would I expect any different?

There's this one stale joke that every comic on the Black Comedy Network has a version of and I used to get a real kick out of it. They'd always tell how the local news stations would only interview the ugliest, most ignorant, stupidest sounding, fewest-toothed person they could find in the crowd if the story had to do with black people.

Channel twelve was keeping the tradition alive, and Luther T. Farrell was its latest star.

18

SHARING THE WEALTH

The next morning I called Sparky.

"City morgue, you stab 'em, we slab 'em."

"Hey, Sparky. It's me."

"Baby! You still calling the little people? After I saw you styling and profiling on channel twelve and saw the article about you in the *Journal* I didn't think you'd have time for your old boy."

"You saw the news, huh?"

"Yeah, baby, I blinked and missed ninety percent of the interview but I saw the other half of it real good."

"And?"

"And what was wrong with your lips? You looked like my cousin Andre looks when he needs to hit a forty."

"I don't know. And did you see all the pimples they put on my face?"

"Yeah, I guess that endorsement contract you were

gonna get with the Oil of Olay folks is out the window now, huh? But look at it like this, I bet Pizza Hut is gonna be calling soon. I can't explain it but ever since I saw you on the news I've had a strange craving for a large pizza Supreme, heavy on the black olives."

Oh, someday I'd pay him back for that.

"Listen, Sparky, I'ma need your help. Have you got a good suit?"

"Is that some kind of trick question? You know I do."

"I'm not talking about that flooding polyester houndstooth mess you've worn to every dance since sixth grade, either."

"Oh, that's cold!"

"Pay attention, I'm trying to take care of you, can you get here in fifteen minutes?"

"I gotta wear my suit? If so we got a problem, it's, uh, at the cleaners right now."

"Which means it's wadded up in a drawer, right?"

"Something like that."

"Don't worry about it, we're going to give that suit to Shayla's daddy and let him bury it, if you hurry over I'm gonna get you a good suit."

"On my way, Mr. Three-peat."

I went into the dayroom and cut off the TV.

"Listen up, general announcement. Who wants to go to the mall for ice cream?"

Four hands shot up.

"OK, go get your going-out clothes on, and get in line."

I went down to my bedroom. Chester X was in his bed, eyes closed.

228

"You up, Mr. X?"

His eyes popped open.

"Hello, Luther. Time for a shave?"

"Very funny. Come on, get dressed, we gotta go out."

I went back upstairs to the kitchen and looked in the Sarge's secret hiding place where she kept all her keys. She kept them at the back of the cupboard over the fridge, in a six-year-old box of Special K. I guess she figured no one in the world would ever look in a box of Special K, not even when it's fresh, so this was the perfect hiding place.

By the time I got to the dayroom everyone was ready to roll.

Sparky was at the front door as we headed out to the bus.

He stopped and said, "So what's this?"

"We're going to the mall for ice cream."

"This is what you need me to do, babysit these folks with you? In public?"

"It's your choice, if you don't want a suit . . ."

"A suit from the mall, right? I mean you aren't planning on detouring me to the Goodwill, are you?"

"A suit from Sleet-Sterling. Designer Exclusives."

"For real? Designer Exclusives? Oh, snap, you drive a hard bargain, bruh."

We all got into the bus.

I had to tell Sparky a hundred times as we headed to the mall that I wasn't going to get him a used suit.

I pulled up to the store's valet parking and unloaded everybody.

I peeled a fifty off my roll from the Sarge's safety deposit box and told the valet, "Keep her near the front, would you, we won't be too long." I'd always wanted to say something like that!

He turned the fifty over, laughed and said, "You got it, chief."

"All right, everyone, fall in." The Crew hooked arms and we paraded through Sleet-Sterling. Sparky hung back a little, trying to act like he wasn't with us. The way he was following us three aisles over made him look just like the half-slick security guard who was trailing us two aisles over.

When we got to the ice cream shop I pulled my knot out of my pocket and slapped a hundred-dollar bill on the counter. I told the woman, "Double scoops for everyone."

She didn't look too happy. She called to the back for help.

Sparky's eyes bugged when he saw the roll.

He said, "Oh my God, my fantasy has come true! My boy has robbed a bank, lost his mind and is taking me on a spending spree before they send him to the joint!"

He told the woman, "Me first! Butter pecan on the top and bubble gum delight on the bottom! And load that baby till it's busting at the seams!"

She pulled out a cone and Sparky said, "Hold on there, you don't understand, darlin', we're going all the way. Sugar cones for everybody!"

The Crew broke out in cheers.

Between everyone picking their own flavors and spilling and wiping faces and having to go to the bathroom and washing up we spent an hour in the food court.

I had them hook up again and we headed over to

Athlete's Outpost. Sparky was always a store or two behind us, pretending he didn't know who we were.

When we got to the sporting goods store Sparky said, "Now, you do remember why I'm here, don't you? You do remember something about a suit from Designer Exclusives at Sleet-Sterling, right? Not that I wouldn't take it, but I mean we aren't talking about a jogging suit, are we?"

"Sparky, you know you're my boy, and I'm not trying to be funny, but before we get you a suit I thought we should stop here. I'm sick of them calling you Ali when we play ball."

"What's wrong with them calling me Ali? They call me that out of respect, after Muhammad Ali, 'cause I float like a butterfly and "—he pretended he was shooting one of his patented weak jump shots—"Bam! I sting like a bee!"

"Naw, man, it doesn't have a thing to do with *that* Ali, it's got to do with your shoes."

The only basketball shoes Sparky ever had were his big brother Jerome's old used shoes, which wasn't a problem except that Jerome wore a size fourteen and Sparky's foot was a ten. By the time they got passed to Sparky, Jerome's old shoes were so big and beat up that it wasn't too long before they started curling up at the toes.

Sparky said, "They been cracking on my shoes?"

"Like you didn't know."

"I swear I didn't. So why they call me Ali?"

"Have you ever checked out Ali Baba's shoes? You seen how the toes curl up at the tips?"

Sparky said, "Oh my God. My own people stabbing me in the back. We can't have that, can we?"

"That's just what I was thinking."

"So we're gonna go in here and get me a pair of size tens?"

"You read my mind, but I was thinking three pairs."

"I love you, bruh!"

Somehow it didn't seem fair that only Sparky was going to get new shoes. An hour later the whole Crew was sporting two-hundred-dollar Air Jordans. As we left everybody scuffed their feet on the floor, sounding like the Detroit Pistons tearing down the court on one of their half-fast breaks.

I stopped at the drugstore and picked up two black permanent markers. Then we fast-broke down to Sleet-Sterling.

Sparky said, "Why do I have the feeling we're not going to be hitting the bargain basement?"

"Because you know it's only the best for my partner and my crew. We're headed upstairs to Designer Exclusives."

Sparky squealed like he'd been hit with a defective lawn mower blade.

As soon as we walked into Men's Designer Exclusives we were attacked by a snotty little woman who acted like something was stinking around her.

"Uh, may I help you, sir?"

"Yeah, we need to look at some suits."

She rolled her eyes and relaxed a little.

"Oh. Well. I'm sure these clothes aren't what you're looking for. You probably want Penney's, it's at the other end of the mall, or Kmart across the street."

"Oh. Do you work on commission here?"

"Of course."

"Good. Is Mr. Brandon in?"

She couldn't hide her surprise that I knew the manager of the department. Mr. Brandon had moved up from managing Thrifty Living.

"He's quite busy in the office —"

"Fine, we'll just browse until he can come out. Gentlemen, find a suit you like."

She gasped and picked up the phone. I heard her whisper something about a couple of hoodlums and a pack of retards.

The back door opened and Ricardo Brandon came out.

He saw me and smiled. "Mr. Farrell, I wasn't expecting to see you." He noticed the Crew rummaging through the suits. "Whoa! You brought everybody. What's up?"

"They've got a party coming up and my mom wants them to be super-sharp. We need some designer suits."

Ricardo was cool, he didn't miss a beat. He said, "Come on in the office with me for a second, Mr. Farrell."

He told the little snot, "If Mr. Farrell's friends need anything get it for them."

After he closed the door Ricardo said, "You know since I'm working here now we can't do the same thing with the clothes that we used to do at Thrifty Living, Luther. If you buy suits and have them altered there's no way I can take them back."

I said, "She told me that, but all the big shots and head honchos are going to be at this party and she wants everyone to be beyond perfect. Something to do with her being close to winning the Adult Foster Care Home of the Year

233

Award. So she wanted to throw a little business your way here, hoping that you could give us something off."

"Designer suits? And she's paying for them? No refunds next week?"

"That's right, suits, shirts, shoes, and ties, too. I know it sounds crazy but that's what she said, she told me to break this off for you, if you can do something about the price."

I handed him three hundred-dollar bills.

"How many suits are we looking at?"

"Six. No, wait, you better make it two for Sparky, and I might as well get one for me, too." I mean if Darnell Dixon got ahold of me I wouldn't have to let Shayla's dad decide what I'd wear in the end. "So make it eight of 'em. All Armanis."

"Eight Armanis?"

"She's lost her mind."

"Hold on. I'ma guesstimate the cost of some sharp accessories and shoes."

He punched a bunch of numbers into a calculator.

"How's fifteen percent off sound?"

"Not as good as twenty."

"You are definitely your mother's son."

"Ouch."

"All right, twenty percent off will kill me, but let's do it."

I said, "Two other things. First, I need the alterations done now, and second, I want you to handle everything, no commission to Miss Thang out there."

"I got no problem with that, Luther, but the tailors can't possibly—"

I peeled another hundred off the roll.

Ricardo smiled and said, "How's two hours sound? But nothing beyond cuffs and waists, you can bring them back later for anything else."

"Sounds like a winner."

"How are you paying?"

I waved the Happy Neighbor Group Homes Inc. checkbook at him.

"Ooh, I thought you were going to peel some more cash off that roll, Luther. I'm afraid company policy is that I have to get an OK from ChekChek on anything this large, looks like we're talking somewhere in the neighborhood of twenty, twenty-five thousand dollars."

"Ricardo, I'm crushed. You know that check's good. ChekChek away, my brother."

The check cleared.

"Didn't doubt it for a minute, Mr. Farrell, but you understand."

Sparky decided he was gonna be troublesome. Since the Crew had picked Armanis he had to have something by someone else. He picked out a bad double-breasted Canali.

I said, "Wait, you remember that 1-800-SUE-EM-ALL brother?"

Sparky said, "Yeah, now when I find me someone to sue and go to court I'll be looking good!"

I said, "Not as good as you will with this." I'd found a suit just like the Versace that Dontay Gaddy was wearing in the commercial, it had been reduced thirty-three percent.

Sparky said, "Oh my God! Oh yeah, put this Canali back!"

"Why should we put it back? Get both of 'em."

Sparky was truly touched.

Two hours later me, the whole Crew and Sparky'd all been fitted and Ricardo started putting their suits in garment bags.

I told him, "Hold on a minute, Ricardo."

I opened the two black permanent markers I'd bought from the drugstore. I handed Sparky one. The Sarge would've brought so much pain on Ricardo that he'd had to take these clothes back, so I had to close this one last door.

Right in front of Ricardo, I started writing everyone's name in big black letters on the inside of their jackets and slacks.

He laughed and said, "Thank you so much, I just knew she'd've figured out some way to make me give her a refund, but looks like that's out now!"

That got Sparky's attention. Quick as he could he wrote "Property of Sparky and the Flint F.D." on the inside of both of his suits.

They all wanted their names on their new gym shoes too so after I'd taken care of that we squeaked, squealed and ran another beautiful fast break back to valet parking.

The bus was at the front door. After we got in I told Sparky, "You know how everything's got a price?"

He hugged his suit bags closer to his chest. "Go ahead, I been expecting this."

"Here's the price of three pairs of shoes and a Canali and a Versace suit. When we get home I'm not going to stick around for when the Sarge gets back. I'm heading out, I took all this cash out of her safety deposit box."

236

"You did what!" Sparky jumped out of his seat, threw the suits on the floor like they were on fire, kicked at the boxes of Air Jordans like they were three pit bulls attacking him and shouted, "Oh no. Turn this bus around and take me back to the mall! How was I supposed to know you stole this from your momma? I thought you stole it from a civilian! Are you crazy? Don't you know what she's gonna have Darnell Dixon do to you?"

I said, "I took it from her safety deposit box but it's what she owes me, it's my education fund. Besides, remember what we used to say, 'Womb to tomb, birth to earth.' "

"Uh-uh, you turn this bus around now! I'm giving all this stuff back!"

"Like they're gonna let you return something with your name all over it in permanent black ink."

"Aw, naw, Luther! What I ever do to you that you'd put me in something bad like this?"

"Hey. You said you wanted a suit."

"But I swear on a stack of Bibles I didn't know it was your momma's money. I never would've done it." Sparky started breathing real deep. "This just ain't right, bruh, what am I gonna do?" He flopped back into the seat and covered his face with his hands.

"You're gonna listen to what I'ma tell you. Like I said, when the Sarge gets home I'ma be gone."

Sparky took a deep breath and said through his fingers, "Now that's the first thing you've said that makes any sense."

"Yeah, I'ma be gone, but you're gonna be there."

Sparky jumped to the front door of the bus and started

237

trying to pry the doors apart. "Open these doors now!" There was no way in the world he could get them open. When I ordered the bus I got the No Tamper Front Door Locking option.

"Listen, Sparky, I gotta have someone watch the Crew while I take care of some business. I know it's a lot to ask, but you're my boy. Who else can I trust to do this for me? And you know you look G'd up in those suits."

"Naw, Luther, she's gonna go Flint on you when she sees what you bought these folks, and who knows what's gonna happen when she finds out you stole from her. I don't know about you, but I ain't got no plans to be spending the rest of my life looking over my shoulder for Darnell Dixon."

I took my wad out and counted ten hundred-dollar bills.

"This is a down payment, you do what I tell you and I'll give you another two thousand later. I'll call Mr. Foster to make sure you stayed till the Sarge and Darnell got back, then I'll drop your cash.

"I've thought the whole thing out. All you gotta do is tell her I called you and asked you to watch the house while I took the Crew out. Little Chicago is going to be coming over later on and he'll take over. You can claim you don't know anything about any of this, and I'm not gonna tell you where I'm going because I don't want them to scare it out of you."

Saying "scare" sounded a lot better than what I meant, "torture."

I said, "Come back tomorrow morning at eight and stay until midnight, then come back on Friday till the Sarge gets back. That's all you gotta do for three thousand dollars cash. That's it."

He looked at the little pile of suits and shoes and then at the cash in his hand and I thought my boy was going to break down.

He said, "It's like you said, no one's gonna take any of this back. I guess I could have all your crew hide their new threads till I got away. If they ever did call me out on it I guess I could say I don't know nothing about none of this."

I said, "The way I'm gonna handle this you won't have to worry, no one's gonna be calling nobody out. I wouldn't leave you hanging."

Sparky looked very serious. "Yeah, I did look sharp in those suits, didn't I? Especially that double-breasted Versace. Dontay Orlando Gaddy didn't have a thing on me, did he?"

"Not a thing."

"Huh," Sparky said, "this just might work out after all. Two thousand more dollars, you say, and all I gotta do is stay there till your momma gets back?"

"Soon as Mr. Foster tells me you stayed the whole time I'll mail it. Besides, when you known me to lie?"

Sparky sighed as he bent over to put the shoes back in their boxes and pick up his garment bags. I guess hanging out with me had had some kind of effect on him. He sounded almost philosophical when he said, "You know, you go through your days kinda wondering what you're really worth, wondering what you'd risk your life for. Now I know; a Canali, a Versace, three pairs of Air Jordans and three thousand dollars cash."

He sounded depressed when he said, "If you'd've asked me before I'da swore up and down that I was worth a lot more than that."

239

"Don't look at it like that, look at it like you're getting paid something around nine thousand dollars for two and a half days' work."

He smiled again. "I guess that does make me sound a whole lot more valuable, doesn't it? I guess you got me over a barrel, let's make this work."

"You're my boy, Sparky."

Sparky turned around and pointed a finger at Mr. Baker. "Now, I ain't as unreasonable as Luther. If you want a smoke we can work something out. You keep your drawers clean until Little Chicago gets home, you hear me?"

Mr. Baker said, "Hey, buddy, I'm feeling a strong urge to smoke."

Sparky said, "You be cool. You're gonna have all the cigarettes you can handle, I swear 'fore God."

The countdown had started to get serious. The Sarge and Darnell would be back from Washington in no time at all. So far, so good.

19

THE LAST LIST AND TESTAMENT OF LUTHER T. FARRELL

I used one of the last pages in my student planner Musings section to make another one of my Luther T. Farrell lists. I had to knock this one out real quick to make sure I didn't miss anything.

I wrote across the top of the page "LUTHER'S LAST LIST," then put:

1. The Happy Neighbor Group Home for Men bus.
2. Quickee Print.
3. Back to the bank.
4. Whittier Middle School.
    a. Transcripts.
    b. Award pickup!!!
    c. Farewell, My Love. Part One.
5. Dealing with Darnell Dixon.
6. Halo Burger.

7. Chester X and Luther T ride again.

8. Farewell, My Love, the Sequel.

1. THE HAPPY NEIGHBOR GROUP HOME FOR MEN BUS.

Getting rid of this bus was going to be easy for me.

A lot of the time people get real attached to their rides and have sick feelings for them. Like the perverted love Darnell Dixon has for his Riviera. But for some reason me and this bus had never bonded. I was so excited when I first got it because I thought I'd have to be fighting the women off, but that never happened.

I think the brothers at school haven't been giving the young women of Flint enough credit and respect when they say most of them are materialistic and nothing but sack-chasers. I can tell you from personal experience that not one girl from Whittier Middle School was the least bit interested in being seen in my bus.

Even though it cost over $85,000.

Even though it's got a DVD player in it.

Even though it's got the No Tamper Front Door option where the most berserk person in the world couldn't bust out.

Even though it's got a bunch of red flashing lights.

Even though it's got HAPPY NEIGHBOR GROUP HOMES INC. written across the sides and on the back in big black letters.

Even with all that going for it there was no way you could call my bus a honey magnet. You have to give the young sisters of Flint their props, they weren't so shallow that all they wanted from a brother was a cool ride. I'm living proof of that.

I got the Sarge's spare keys, moved Darnell's Riviera and drove the bus back to Big Bob's Camper and RV World.

An hour later me and a cashier's check for $47,543 were headed back to the home. Big Bob had really stuck it to me, but I figure this was a quick way to get a bunch of cash together. They gave me a ride back to the home and I started wheeling in Darnell's Rivy.

If the Sarge wanted to be paid back for the bus and the metal box cash she could just deduct them from my education fund, wherever that figment of my imagination was hanging out these days.

One down, seven to go.

2. QUICKEE PRINT.

This was easy too. An hour after I walked in with the weekly receipts briefcase I walked back out with two copies of every document, deed, bankbook, and ledger that the Sarge had hidden in the secret safety deposit box.

Two down, six to go.

3. BACK TO THE BANK.

I took the safety deposit box key and went back to see Elaine. I put back $25,000 of the $50,000 I'd taken and left one set of the Xeroxed copies of everything in the Sarge's safety deposit box. I opened a safety deposit box of my own and put the other set of Xeroxes and the originals in it.

Three down, five to go.

4. WHITTIER MIDDLE SCHOOL.
    a. Transcripts.
    b. Award pickup!!!

I wheeled Darnell's Rivy into Whittier's parking lot. How come there was no one to see me now? It seemed like anytime any kids saw me in my bus, they'd always laugh and point.

I went to the office and asked Mrs. Vickers if my medal had come in.

She said, "You'll have to check with Mr. Brown, he was handling that."

I said to her, "I need to get a copy of my transcripts, too, I'm transferring to another school in another city next September."

She went to a file cabinet and thumbed through some folders.

"Sorry to hear that, young man. By the way, I saw you on the news."

I made a face.

She looked up from the cabinet and said, "Now, that's strange, I can't seem to find your records. I've got a Luther T. Farrell here, but according to this there's no *Loser* T. Farrell enrolled in the school."

All the rejects and lowlifes who worked in the office and all the fools that had been sent down here to get disciplined died laughing.

Mrs. V said, "Sorry, sweetheart, I just couldn't resist."

She started Xeroxing my transcripts.

"That'll be twenty dollars for this copy and twenty dollars for the copy we'll have to send directly to your new school, Luther. What's the address?"

"I'll have to email you when I know it. Can I talk to Mr. Brown now?"

She said, "Just a minute, he has someone in there."

I peeked over her shoulder into Brown's office. Some poor soul was stuck in that tiny chair while Brown pretended to be on the phone.

Finally he held his hand over the mouthpiece and said to the student, "You should've thought of that before. Enjoy your time in detention."

Some stupid seventh grader came mumbling out of the office.

Brown signaled to Mrs. V.

As soon as I got into the office he pointed at the chair.

He must be crazy. I just stood there.

He finally looked up to see why I hadn't followed his orders.

He put his hand over the mouthpiece again and said, "Right there, it just came in. Congratulations."

I picked up my medal and couldn't help smiling.

4.   WHITTIER MIDDLE SCHOOL
     c. Farewell, My Love. Part One.

I kind of floated down to Ms. Warren's class. I knew this was her free period and I hoped she'd be in her room correcting papers or something.

I knocked on her door.

"Come in."

I walked in and there she sat, looking like she just fell out of the pages of *Essence* magazine.

"Luther!"

"Hey, Ms. Warren."

"Is something wrong? Why'd you and Sparky skip my class?"

"Everything's cool. I just wanted to come say goodbye. I'm going to be moving to another city today."

"You know that's the trouble with you ninth graders, you all grow up to be tenth graders and leave us like we meant nothing to you."

"No, Ms. Warren, it's not like that. I just wanted to come and tell you that you really helped me a lot, you got me using lists and I can see how helpful they are with everything. That's one of the things that got me organized for the science fairs."

"Luther, you don't have to thank me, it was a pleasure having you as a student. If I didn't think it would embarrass you to death I'd give you a silver star to put on your forehead."

We both laughed.

She said, "I saw you on TV the other night."

"I know. I looked like a real idiot. They cut all the good parts out. The only good thing about it was that it was only on for a hot second."

She said, "On channel twelve?"

I nodded.

She said, "At eleven o'clock?"

"No, I saw it at six."

"They must not've shown the whole thing. At eleven

246

they did a very good report and you sounded very intelligent. You seemed a little nervous at first, but who wouldn't? They even had a statement from the mayor's office saying that because of you there was going to be a full investigation. He even thanked you for bringing this problem to light. You didn't see any of that?"

"No, all I saw was me licking my lips and saying, 'Nope,' 'yup,' and 'uh-huh.' "

Ms. Warren laughed. "Too bad you missed it, you were most impressive."

"Really?"

She laughed again. "I was overcome by your brilliance."

I can't believe how fine Ms. Warren is! If I was a little older or she was a little younger she'd be in some deep trouble.

"Anyway, Ms. Warren, I gotta go. Thank you for all of your help and for making me feel like I can do anything."

She said, "Luther T. Farrell, you get out of this room before you make me cry."

She stood up and hugged me. I don't know how long I held on to her but after a while she started doing that squirming that women do when they want you to know that you're making them uncomfortable and if you don't quit pretty soon there're going to be hurt feelings involved. I let her go and left her room and her life.

Four down, four to go.

5. DEALING WITH DARNELL DIXON.

Darnell Dixon knew he'd crossed the line. It wasn't like he'd done it accidentally, either, like he'd kind of just brushed a toe or two over. Uh-uh, what he'd done was a deliberate, Olympic-record-breaking, four-hundred-yard kangaroo-leap over the line. His words about the Sarge just couldn't be ignored or allowed to bounce off my mind of steel, there had to be some kind of payback.

I mean his slam about the condoms was pretty weak. But she is my momma and some respect is called for.

It wasn't like Darnell had been brought up in Utah or somewhere like that, he was a stone-cold Flintstone born and raised, so he had to know better than to play the dozens, it was the principle of the thing.

So once again it was lesson time and I knew the best way to cause Mr. Darnell Dixon pain. It was sitting in the parking lot shiny as a cue ball in the sun.

Was I going to slash his tires?

Nah. Childish and easily fixed by his insurance company.

Was I going to key his paint job?

No, no, no. Even though I knew some pretty funny things I could scratch in the paint.

Was I going to pour sugar in his gas tank?

Uh-uh. Too stupid a trick for what he'd done. Besides, I don't know if that really works.

Was I going to hide a dead fish under his backseat as a little natural air freshener?

Nope. The way he kept that Rivy Dog so clean, he'd find it before the corpse even had a chance to draw three flies.

Was I going to hop in his car, go to the Secretary of State's office, whip my power-of-attorney form out and sign the Sarge's name and have the car put into my name at the same time I had those weak HI BABY license plates changed?

Hmmm, sounds like a winner to me.

With one quick signature the Riviera went from being Darnell Dixon's Certified Love Machine on Wheels to Luther T. Farrell's Philosophy Mobile! The car blue-booked at $20,000 so with that and the cash and the funds from the bus it came up to me taking $92,000, my education fund.

Five down, three to go.

6. HALO BURGER.

I drove into Halo Burger's lot and saw Bo's bike chained to the Dumpster. So far, so good.

It was even better news when I walked into the lobby and saw P.D. wiping tables. Great! I wouldn't have to talk to Bo.

I said, "P.D., what's happening?"

He turned around and gave me a hug. "Luther! Good to see you again!"

"Yeah, good to see you, too. Is Bo working today?"

He said, "Oh yeah, pretty darn nice guy, that Bo Travis. I'll go get him for you."

"No! I gotta bounce. Could you give him this package for me?"

"You know me, Luther, when I say I'm gonna do something I do it."

"Cool." I handed P.D. the small box I put together for Bo.

"I'll get it right to him."

"Anyway, P.D., you take care of yourself."

"You too, Luther. I saw you on TV, I told my roommates you usually don't look that scared unless your mom's after you."

"See you later, P.D."

I was getting ready to pull out on Saginaw when a loud bang came from the trunk.

Bo Travis walked up to the driver's door. I got out.

He tapped the box I'd given to P.D. and said, "What is this?"

I'm getting pretty good at coming up with stories real quick. I said, "It's hush money. My mother saw all those magnets you had from Dontay Orlando Gaddy and she's scared to death of him. She figured you were gonna put a suit in on her so she was hoping you'd settle out of court."

He said, "Tell your momma she doesn't have to worry, no one's gonna sue her, we hadn't paid the rent in three months, we ain't got no cause to sue no one."

I said, "Whatever. She apologizes for what Darnell Dixon did and hopes that cash does something for your pain and suffering." I couldn't believe the way these lies were just popping out!

He said, "Tell her thank you, but I wasn't thinking about—"

I said, "Look, Bo, that's fifteen G in that box, that could get you back in school. And you should just take it for KeeKee. Take it."

He looked at the box, then looked down Saginaw Street. "All right, tell your mother thank you."

"Cool."

"And thank you for bringing me KeeKee's papers, she was really proud of those."

"Be cool, Bo."

Bo gave me some dap.

Six down, two to go.

7. CHESTER X AND LUTHER T RIDE AGAIN.

When I parked my Rivy Dog at the home, Mr. Baker was sitting on the front porch blowing a long stream of smoke up to the sky. A nearly full ashtray sat right next to him.

I walked up and he said, "Don't even think about it, Loser. And I know what I'm saying and I don't have a lisp, neither."

"Whatever, Mr. Baker."

I went inside. Sparky and the Crew were watching *The A-Team*. Chester X must still be down in our room.

I said, "Thanks a bunch for keeping an eye on things, Dewey."

My sarcasm didn't mean a thing to him. He said, "I got you covered, bruh."

I called Mr. Baker in, turned off the TV and, ignoring all the groans and grumbling, said, "OK, general announcement." To make sure I had everyone's attention I stood in front of the TV.

"I've got some bad news. Today is the last day I'm going to be working here."

I didn't expect tears or anything, but some kind of reaction would've been nice.

Mr. Baker said, "OK. Now what's the bad news?"

Mr. Foster said, "That *is* bad news, Luther. Who'll be our next aide?"

I said, "My mother will get someone in."

Mr. Foster said, "Oh dear."

Sparky said, "My man, you finally got up the nerve to quit! I guess in light of your recent felonies you're gonna be taking it on the lam, huh? Your timing couldn't've been better. Jerome just got sentenced to two years so there's lots of space at my crib."

I told him, "Thanks, Sparky, but I'm moving down south."

He said, "What?"

I said, "For real. I can't let you know yet where I'm moving, but once I get there I'll call you."

Sparky really looked hurt. He said, "Oh, so that's what you meant when you said you weren't going to be here when your momma got back? You planning on moving away? You're just gonna up and go without telling your boy about it?"

"Sparky, what choice do I have?"

"What happened to 'womb to tomb, birth to earth'? How you just gonna leave me here in Flint? You know I'll come with you if you want me to."

I said, "You know I want you to. Look, I'ma need three months to get set up where I'm going."

He said, "What? Three months? What's that supposed to mean?"

I said, "Trust me. I got it all thought out, you'll be old enough by then to legally leave home. Once I'm settled

in you can come down with me, I swear it and word
is bond."

"Three months, huh?"

"Make sure you save enough of that cash for a bus
ticket."

Sparky said, "Bus ticket nothing, I'm putting five hundred aside to fly outta Bishop. And I'm not flying regular,
neither, I'ma get me a seat in coach, baby!"

Mr. Baker said, "This is all very touching, this is like
something out of *The Bold and the Beautiful.* If you need me
I'll be on the porch smoking."

Mr. Foster kept going, "Oh dear."

I said, "Don't worry, Mr. Foster, I'm sure she'll get someone good to take over."

He said, "Ah, you have more faith in the woman than
I do. I keep seeing us being left to the tender mercies of
Darnell Dixon and Little Chicago. Oh dear."

I said, "I don't think so. She knows she's got to keep you
happy, she knows she's gotta keep this place running
smooth. She may seem coldhearted but she's not stupid."

Mr. Foster said, "Oh dear."

I said, "Let me go get Chester X, we've got to get on the
road."

Sparky said, "What's that?"

I said, "I'm taking Chester X with me."

Sparky said, "What? You're taking him and leaving me?
How come that dinosaur gets to go now and I have to wait
three months?"

"That's just the way it's gotta be, Sparky. If it wasn't for him I wouldn't have anywhere to go. *We* wouldn't have anywhere to go."

He said, "I'ma trust you on this, bruh, but it's looking pretty shaky to me. Are you sure you got my address for that other two G you owe me?"

"When you ever known me to lie?"

I went into the basement.

Chester X was reading the paper. He said, "Flint's latest star, how are you?"

I said, "Mr. X, if we leave now and drive twenty-four straight hours we can be in Port Saint Lucie by this time to-morrow. Otherwise we can take a couple of days, but either way we're outta here in fifteen minutes."

Chester X sagged like he'd done when I busted him with the pills. He started crying and said, "Oh, thank you, Luther, thank you!"

I said, "Get your Armani and your bathroom stuff to-gether. Leave everything else, we'll shop as we go."

He said, "Luther, you have no idea how grateful I am."

I said, "Mr. X, it's as much for me as it is for you."

Chester X said, "I'm glad you feel that way, 'cause I might've been exaggerating a little about the friendliness of Florida women, I wouldn't want you to be disappointed."

"Oh no, Mr. X, if I don't have four or five honeys within the first week we're turning around and coming right back to Flint."

He said, "And I'll hate to see you go, but I will wish you a happy return home."

We each packed one little bag. All I had was my CDs, my new suit, some other clothes, my musings journal, and my three, hey-hey-hey!, gold medals. I left my magazine collection under the mattress.

I carried the suitcases upstairs and Chester X carried the suits.

Chester X said, "I want to say goodbye to everyone, Luther."

We went into the dayroom.

Chester X shook everyone's hand.

Sparky said to Mr. X, "You know that's my spot you got. You sure you wouldn't want to wait for three months, then come down?"

Chester X said, "Back off, Spunky, we're on a mission."

When we went on the front porch Mr. Baker blew out another long jet of smoke and said, "See you later, Loser. We're under new management, and things are definitely looking up!" Seven down, one to go.

8. FAREWELL, MY LOVE, THE SEQUEL.

I parked the newly christened Philosophy Mobile in front of Shayla's home next to the Patrick House of Mortuary.

"I'm just going to be a minute, Mr. X, I've got to say goodbye to someone."

"Luther, you take your time, son, the seats in this car are like sitting in the couch in someone's living room. Don't worry if I doze off."

"You just try to stay awake, I won't be long."

I took three giant breaths, told myself how confident I was and knocked on Shayla's door.

Her mom answered, looking just as fine as ever.

"Luther, come on in."

"Hello, Mrs. Patrick, I'm not going to stay, I just want to talk to Shayla for a minute."

"She and her dad have gone down to Detroit to see the Tigers, Luther."

"The *Tigers?*"

Mrs. Patrick said, "I know, but it's been a tradition for years. They won't be back until late. Should I have her call you when they get in? It probably won't be until after eleven."

In a strange way I was kind of relieved. I didn't know if I'd actually be able to apologize to Shayla without ruining it by saying something derogatory about her at the same time.

I was also kind of sad. I really should've told Shayla when I had all those chances. It's like that great philosopher, whose name escapes me at the moment, once said, "He who hesitates is lost."

"No," I said to Mrs. Patrick, "I just wanted to say goodbye to Shayla and give her something."

"Goodbye?"

"Uh, yeah, I'm moving down south to live with my granddad."

"Oh no! I know Shayla's going to be very disappointed that she wasn't here."

Sometimes words jump out of your mouth before you can control them. I said, "Really?" And I didn't say it in a neutral way, either, that one word was dripping with desperation and eyes-wide-open-stupidity when I said it.

Mrs. Patrick said, "I know I shouldn't tell you this, Luther, but Shayla has always had something of a crush on you."

"Really?" This time my voice cracked, something it hasn't done in a good six or seven days.

She laughed. "If only you knew. But you never heard that from me."

Women! Leave it to one of them to have these strong feelings for a brother but not to have the courage to let him know.

Hmmm, maybe I could stay here in Flint after all, maybe I could live on the north side somewhere where the Sarge doesn't own any houses . . . then I thought about what Darnell was going to do when he found out that I'd repoed his Rivy Dog and I knew even the love of a good woman wasn't enough to keep me here.

I said, "Well, I've always kinda liked her, too."

She said, "Yes, Luther, we've all known that. So is your mother closing her businesses?"

I told her, "No, she's staying here while I look after Granddad." I changed the subject. "Could you give Shayla this for me?"

I handed her last year's science fair gold medal.

"What's this?"

"It's really Shayla's, it's from last year and they gave it to me by mistake."

Mrs. Patrick looked from the medal to me and said, "I don't understand."

I started walking back down the front porch steps. I said, "She'll know what it means, but tell her it's a straight-up trade, she's got to send me the silver one."

Mrs. Patrick followed me to the sidewalk. "Does she have your new address?"

"Not yet, I'm not exactly sure where we'll be, but I've got her email and I'll write to her once I know."

"Luther, if there's anything that we can do please don't hesitate to call."

She looked in the front seat of the Rivy and said, "Oh my God!"

Chester X was stone asleep. His face was mashed into the window and his mouth was wide open. You could see his gums, his tonsils and halfway down his throat.

"Oh," I said, "that's my granddad, he's not dead, I can see his breath steaming up the window."

Mrs. Patrick said, "You know what, Luther? I am so glad that Shayla's father isn't here right now, I know if he saw this he'd make the most horribly inappropriate comment you could ever imagine."

She laughed and said, "Luther, I want you to call me once you get there. I'm not real comfortable with this. I'm going to be worried until I hear from you. And I know Shayla will want to say goodbye."

I said, "I promise, Mrs. Patrick. I'll call you in a couple of days."

She opened her arms and I walked into them.

This was very uncool. It was probably because I had some sadness about leaving Flint, or because I wouldn't be watching TV with my crew again, or because I wouldn't be seeing Shayla Queen of the Damned Patrick for a long time, but something about Mrs. Patrick's hug was making me want to hold on and cry.

I held Shayla's mom way past that time that most

women do that squirming-uncomfortable thing, but she never did. She didn't even give me those little doggie pats on the back to let me know the hug should be ending soon, she just let me hold her.

Finally I let go.

She said, "I'll be waiting for your call, Luther. You really should talk to Shayla, too."

I pulled myself together and said, "No joke, Mrs. Patrick, I'll call in a couple of days."

I jumped into the Riviera and headed out to I-75, a road that runs all the way from Michigan to Florida. And if that's not a sign I don't know one when I see it.

As I pulled onto the expressway I couldn't help thinking of that great philosopher, whose name escapes me at the moment, who once said, "He who fights and runs away lives to fight another day."

Turning up the radio in the Philosophy Mobile to muffle my new granddad's snoring, I put the seat all the way back, got a little lean going on and hit the cruise control.

And I left Flint behind.

About the Author

Christopher Paul Curtis is the bestselling author of *Bud, Not Buddy*, winner of the Newbery Medal and the Coretta Scott King Author Award, among many other honors. His first novel, *The Watsons Go to Birmingham—1963*, was also singled out for many awards, among them a Newbery Honor and a Coretta Scott King Honor. Christopher Paul Curtis grew up in Flint, Michigan. After high school he went to work on the assembly line at Fisher Body Flint Plant No. 1 while attending the Flint branch of the University of Michigan, where he began to write essays and fiction. He is now a full-time writer. He and his wife, Kay, have two children and live in Windsor, Ontario, Canada.

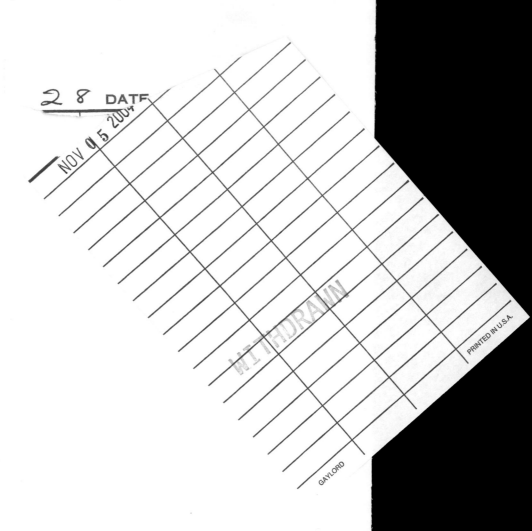